To Tempt A
WOLF
KATE STEELE

ELLORA'S CAVE
ROMANTICA PUBLISHING

$\mathscr{W}$hat the critics are saying...

ဆာ

4 1/2 Hearts "This author is very good at combining romance, erotica, and suspense into a story that is very hard to put down. The characters are very real despite their supernatural aspects, and the story has enough twists and turns and hot love scenes to keep a reader very interested."

~ *The Romance Studio*

An Ellora's Cave Romantica Publication

www.ellorascave.com

To Tempt a Wolf

ISBN 9781419959127
To Tempt a Wolf Copyright © 2006 Kate Steele
Edited by Heather Osborn.
Cover art by Syneca.

This book printed in the U.S.A. by Jasmine–Jade Enterprises, LLC.

Electronic book Publication November 2006
Trade paperback Publication August 2009

This book is a work of fiction and any resemblance to persons, living or dead, or places, events or locales is purely coincidental. The characters are productions of the author's imagination and used fictitiously.

TO TEMPT A WOLF

Trademarks Acknowledgement

∞

The author acknowledges the trademarked status and trademark owners of the following wordmarks mentioned in this work of fiction:

BMW: Bayerische Motoren Werke Aktiengesellschaft

Corvette: General Motors

Prologue

ဢ

Hayley Royden was restless. Tired from the time she'd spent traveling to visit her sister Bryn, she'd gone to bed early, hoping to crash for the night. A couple of hours later she woke, punched her pillow and knew there'd be no going back to sleep for a while. That was one of the problems associated with being a night owl. Going to bed early rarely worked. That, plus finding herself in an unfamiliar bed, had caused her to jolt awake.

She went for the book she'd stashed in one of her bags, deciding a little romance and intrigue would be the very thing. As she crossed the floor, a board creaked underfoot. She paused and heard a scrabbling noise and some muffled laughter from down the hall. Apparently Bryn and her fiancé Logan were just making their way to bed.

Hayley picked up the book, absently staring at the cover as her mind considered Bryn and Logan. Her smile was wistful as she thought about her own lack of a love life. Why could she never meet the right guy? She focused on the book and decided it wouldn't do. After quietly dressing, she walked down the hall and descended the stairs. She made her way through the darkened house with the aid of the little flashlight she always carried on her keychain. The kitchen was just ahead, and if she remembered correctly, there was a door that led out into the backyard.

As she let herself out, she breathed a sigh of relief and contentment. The night air was cool and fresh and she felt her spirits lift as she walked away from the house into the surrounding woods. The moon, a few days away from being full, rode high in the sky, making it easy for her to see the path that wound through the trees.

Hayley wandered slowly, no destination in mind. She'd always had a good sense of direction and felt at ease with nature. As she followed the path, she heard the soft splash of water in the distance.

Spotting the reflective glint of moonlight, she moved forward until she entered a clearing where a shallow pool of water was fed by a trickling stream. A smile lit her face as she walked to edge of the pond. Kneeling, she trailed her fingers in the clear water. It was warm.

She gave the water a speculative look and then checked the surrounding area. Deciding to go for it, she quickly began to peel out of her clothes and stepped into the welcoming water.

She didn't see the pair of eyes that glowed with a bluish-green incandescence as they watched her lower herself into the pool.

The water was deep enough that she could swim, which she did, taking a few laps around its circumference. Wearying of that exercise, she flipped over on her back and floated, admiring the clear night sky with its moon and myriad stars all shining so brightly. Her body was so relaxed, she stifled a yawn as she found herself missing the bed she'd left not so long ago. With a sigh, Hayley paddled to the edge of the pond and stood, walking from the water.

Hayley was unaware of the picture she presented as the water sluiced from her body, leaving it pale and shimmering under the moonlight. Her honey-blonde hair, slicked back, revealed the pure, lovely features of her face. Tall and lithe, her curves were full and firm. Bounteous breasts were topped by pink nipples that hardened in the cool night air. A trim waist accentuated her generous hips and the sleek curve of taut buttocks. Below her slightly rounded belly, the nest of curls that graced her mound was pale and glistening with water from the pool. Her legs were long and curvaceous, from the tops of her shapely thighs to her slim, arched feet.

Reaching for her clothes, she bent to retrieve her shirt and began to dry herself. A slight rustling sound caught her attention and she searched the darkness until her startled gaze landed on the wolf.

It stood with an air of calm majesty not twenty feet away. Hayley froze in surprise. A slight frisson of fear tightened her belly, until she remembered all the things she had read about wolves. One researcher in particular had said that wolves did not commonly attack humans and that during her study of them, the wolves, especially the males, had been curious about her and had often spent hours near her, seemingly studying her as she'd studied them.

She strove to relax her tightened muscles as she admired the wolf. Its fur was thick and sleek, mostly black, growing lighter toward the chest, underbelly and legs. It seemed huge, although she had nothing to compare it with, never having seen a wolf before. And its eyes… Were they *glowing*? Surely it was a reflection of the moonlight off the water, she mused. Although unsure of what eye color wolves usually had, she found the bright blue-green quite remarkable.

A wisp of night air blew across her skin, causing her to shiver. "I hope you don't mind," she told the wolf softly, "but I've got to move. I don't have any fur, you know, and it's a little chilly here with no clothes on."

In answer, the wolf cocked his head then sat, staring at her expectantly.

"Guess that means it's okay," Hayley muttered, as she carefully, with smooth easy movements, dressed herself.

All the while, the wolf watched with interest.

Slipping into her shoes, she faced the wolf. "Well, it was nice meeting you," she offered, "but I have to go. Hope you enjoyed the show."

The wolf's mouth opened, his tongue lolling out in a large canine grin.

11

A suspicious frown crossed Haley's face. "Did anyone ever tell you you were strange?" Then she amended, "But very beautiful. Thank you for keeping me company. Maybe we'll meet again some time."

She backed away a few steps, just to see if there was any objection. When the wolf made no move, she turned and followed the trail back to the house. Slipping quietly into the kitchen, she locked the door and crept upstairs to her room, quickly changing and sliding back into bed.

Safe, warm and pleasantly sleepy, Hayley began to drift off as the haunting howl of a wolf pierced the night's quiet. She listened to the sound with awe as a shiver slid down her spine.

* * * * *

Just down the hall, Logan and Bryn both listened to the howl.

"Jace," Logan identified as he wondered what his best friend and fellow alpha was up to.

"What's he doing?" Bryn asked with a sleepy yawn.

Logan hugged her to him. "Probably just out for a run."

"Mmm," Bryn murmured as she snuggled close and went to sleep.

Logan lay awake and listened to a second rolling howl. He'd heard his soon-to-be sister-in-law returning from her moonlight ramble a few minutes ago. He lay quietly, speculating upon the possibilities...

Chapter One

ℬ

Laughter rang in the kitchen as Hayley, Bryn and Logan enjoyed an informal breakfast, seated in chairs around the butcher block-topped island in the middle of the kitchen. Logan had volunteered to cook and made more than passably good omelets accompanied by toast, fresh fruit, coffee and juice. Afterward, he even volunteered to do the cleanup and bade the girls to stay seated. While he worked, he listened to their easy chatter.

"I have to say, Bryn, you sure have found a winner here." At the sink, Logan turned and gave Hayley a grin and a wink. "Steve wouldn't lift a hand to help in the kitchen—just one of the many reasons I broke up with him."

"You broke up with Steve?" Bryn asked incredulously. "I thought you said he was the perfect guy for you."

"Yeah, well, Mr. Perfect turned out to have a few flaws that couldn't be overlooked. Including the fact that he didn't want any more children."

"Oh no, Hay, I'm so sorry."

"It's okay, sis, I found out he's a lousy father." She shifted to include Logan who had turned to listen. "Steve has a daughter from a previous marriage, but he doesn't really want her—he ditches her with his parents at every opportunity. Of course, they're thrilled to have their granddaughter, but even Steve's mom admits that he won't spend time with her."

With a disgusted frown, Logan went back to cleaning the kitchen counter.

"How can anyone neglect their own child that way?" Bryn asked sadly as she sat contemplating the tabletop with a troubled look on her face. Her hand absently rubbed her midsection.

Hayley watched her with growing suspicion, a smile spreading across her face. "Bryn, are you *pregnant*?"

Bryn looked up quickly, meeting Hayley's expectant gaze, then looked to Logan for direction. His expression was blankly neutral. He was leaving the decision in Bryn's hands.

Hayley watched a slow, glowing smile spread across Bryn's face. "Yes," she confessed.

"Oh my God!" Hayley screamed. "This is so wonderful!" She hugged Bryn tight, rocking her with enthusiasm until she realized what she was doing. "I'm rattling you like a cocktail shaker! Don't let me do that," she admonished. Her eyes were bright with tears of happiness as she sprang out of her chair and approached Logan. "Gotta have a hug, big guy," she insisted and wrapped her arms around Logan, bussing him noisily on the cheek.

Logan returned her hug, laughing at Hayley's open enthusiasm.

"Mom and Dad are gonna flip!" she declared as she resumed her seat. "They'll be on cloud nine with their first grandchild. Takes the heat off me, I can tell you," she confessed to Logan as he returned to his chair. "They're constantly at me with the subtle hints about how nice it would be to have a grandchild."

She watched as Logan draped his arm around Bryn's shoulder and pulled her to him, planting a tender kiss on her temple. "I'm glad you approve," he rumbled, the contentment clear in his voice.

Hayley smiled, her eyes stinging with unshed tears.

"Are you okay?" Bryn questioned.

Hayley's smile broadened. "You two love each other," she replied. "It's just so sweet, I'm speechless."

"You're also nuts," Bryn accused fondly.

"That too," Hayley admitted cheerfully, warmed by the sisterly insult. "Come on, Logan, I'll help you finish cleaning up, and you, my dear sister, will stay seated."

"Hayley," Bryn complained, "the baby's not due for eight months—I don't think I need to take it easy yet."

"Nevertheless, I intend to spoil my niece or nephew and I mean to begin now."

* * * * *

After the cleanup was accomplished, Logan went into his den to make some phone calls that pertained to his job.

Hayley wasn't sure exactly what it was Logan did for a living. Bryn had given her some vague explanation of his job as a freelance troubleshooter of sorts.

Despite Bryn's deliberate vagueness, Hayley knew there was more to be explained. She didn't push the issue, knowing her sister would tell her in time. It was one of the advantages of knowing someone your entire life. After a while, you knew things about them just from having spent so much time with them.

Leaving Logan to his work, Hayley accompanied Bryn to her bookstore where she and Clare, Bryn's best friend and business partner, engaged in a noisy and joyous reunion. Bryn's friendship with Clare had spilled over to include Hayley, and the three of them had spent an inordinate amount of time together as they grew up.

The day was spent working and talking as they caught up on each other's news. Hayley was impressed with the bookstore and it was apparent the customers were as well, judging by the number of them that came and went during the course of the day.

As the afternoon wore on, Hayley decided to share a certain bit of news she'd been holding back. After the last customer left and the three of them were engaged in some general straightening before locking up for the night, she walked to the front of the store and stood in front of the new releases section.

"You know," she called out clearly, "my book is going to look real good here."

"And what book would that be, Hay?" Bryn asked with indulgence.

"The erotically charged romantic suspense I wrote that got accepted for publication a few weeks ago."

Bryn watched Hayley's face, looking for the first sign of a teasing smile. None was forthcoming. "You're serious." Bryn looked at Clare. "She's serious." Her incredulous gaze went back to Hayley. "Are you *serious*?"

At her wordless nod, Bryn and Clare rushed forward, enveloping her in a hug. "Congratulations! Why didn't you tell us you were writing a book?" Clare asked.

"Yeah, why didn't you tell us?" Bryn asked accusingly as she gave Hayley another hug and a retaliatory pinch on the arm.

"Ow!" she yelped. "Has Logan found out you're a pincher?"

"Yes," Bryn replied complaisantly. "But don't worry about him. He gets in some pinches of his own."

"I can just imagine," Clare intoned, wiggling her eyebrows suggestively.

Bryn colored as Hayley and Clare snickered. "All right," she admonished. "If you two are through?" She fixed Hayley with a steady look. "Explain, little sister."

Hayley wrinkled her nose at Bryn's big-sister tone. "A few years ago, I had the notion to write a book. You know how much I read." Bryn nodded and Hayley continued. "I wrote a half dozen chapters and lost interest, so I put it away. Then last year, the urge came again, so I dug out the stuff I'd written and read it over." She laughed. "It was horrid!

"I still had the urge though, and what I thought were some really great ideas, so I tried it again. I didn't lose interest this time," she explained enthusiastically, her eyes shining. "In fact, I got addicted. I decided not to tell anyone until the book was finished and I'd submitted it to a publisher. If it got rejected, I'd quietly bury it and maybe try again in a couple more years."

Haley grinned and shrugged a little self-consciously. "It didn't get rejected. So I've bagged my job with Davis Data Systems and I'm going to do the writing thing full time."

"You quit your job?"

"Yeah, Bryn, I really want to do this and I've got plenty of money saved as a backup. You know what a tightwad I am. And I was thinking," she rushed on breathlessly. "Now that you're moving in with Logan, how would you like to rent your house to me? That is, if you don't have other plans for it?"

Hayley watched Bryn closely for her reaction, noting her dazed look. The last thing she wanted to do was upset her sister, especially in her condition, but this was important to her. Hayley felt her whole life was on the verge of a huge change and somehow, moving here to Whispering Springs felt...right.

"Are you okay?" Hayley asked. Her voice was tinged with trepidation. She wanted Bryn's approval.

"I'm fine. I just need to sit down a minute," Bryn answered. They moved to one of the relaxation nooks that were scattered through the store for the convenience of the customers and settled on an overstuffed sofa. "You've taken me by surprise. You've really thought this all out, haven't you?"

Hayley nodded earnestly.

"Okay, if you're sure you want it, the house is yours," Bryn took Hayley's hand. "But you know you're welcome to stay with Logan and me, don't you?"

"Sis, I know you guys would let me stay with you, but that's the *last* thing you need right now. You and Logan are just starting your lives together." Hayley squeezed Bryn's hand. "You don't need your wacky sister living with you."

"You're not wacky," Bryn denied, her lower lip trembling.

Her eyes filling with tears, Hayley gave her a watery grin.

"Now don't you two start blubbering," Clare ordered, taking in the emotion-charged atmosphere. "This is cause for celebration! Little sis is gonna be a famous author and she's coming to live in our town. Can I have your autograph?" she asked with feigned, wide-eyed excitement.

Bryn gave a watery chuckle.

"Do you ever just want to smack her?" Hayley asked Bryn as she gave Clare the evil eye.

Clare drew back in mock horror and the three of them laughed, breaking the tension.

"Let's drive over to the house now," Bryn told them. "There are some things I want to pick up. You can take a look around the place and make sure it's what you want. And if I remember correctly, there's some butter pecan ice cream in the freezer," she said smiling. "We should do something about it, since this is a celebration and all."

With a chorus of eager agreement they locked up and headed over to Bryn's house. Bryn drove with Hayley as a passenger. Clare followed behind in her own car so that she could go straight home when they were done.

As they drove through the town and into the outskirts where Bryn's house was located, Hayley admired the scenery. Whispering Springs was one of those quaint and quiet towns with an interesting, diverse and not-too-big business district. It also contained small suburban neighborhoods where the houses weren't all clones of each other. And they were actually spread far enough apart to allow the residents some privacy.

The yards were neat and carefully kept. Flowers of different kinds grew in orderly and sometimes not-so-orderly fashions in gardens, window boxes and along walkways. Large trees attested to the fact that this place had deep roots and could not be classed as some housing development that sprang up practically overnight. There was a calm and solid feel to the place that sank into her bones and made her feel immediately at home.

Pulling into the driveway next to Bryn's house, Hayley saw a truck was already parked there. It bore a logo on the side that advertised McKenna Designs.

"I wonder what Jace is doing here?" Bryn wondered aloud.

"Who's Jace?"

"Jace McKenna. He's Logan's best friend."

They exited the car and, when Clare joined them, walked up the porch steps to the front door. Bryn tried the door handle. It wasn't locked and she stepped inside.

"Jace?"

"In here," came a slightly muffled reply.

Hayley felt an involuntary shiver slide down her spine. Something about that deep, rich voice struck a chord inside her. The sensation wasn't unpleasant and yet she found it disconcerting to be affected by someone she'd yet to lay eyes on. Her curiosity rose sharply. She and Clare followed Bryn to the kitchen.

Standing in front of the kitchen sink, taking the last spoonful from a container of butter pecan ice cream, was the most gorgeous example of male beauty she'd ever laid eyes on. *Lord, is every man in this town a hunk? Looks like I came to the right place*, she thought as a ripple of anticipatory tension spread through her.

Jace McKenna stood at ease, leaning against the kitchen sink as he finished his ice cream. Standing six feet, four inches tall, he filled out his jeans and t-shirt in a way that instantly drew a woman's notice. Hard, muscular and tight in all the right places.

His ruggedly handsome face was framed by black hair that was short on the sides and longer at the top—a thick glossy wave that gleamed in the sunlight that flooded in through the kitchen windows. Black brows framed sparkling blue-green eyes that were shaded by a thick fringe of black lashes, while a straight nose pointed the way down to lips that invoked thoughts of hot nights filled with sensual kisses. His warm, olive-toned skin was bronzed by the sun.

Jace swept a casual yet friendly eye over Bryn and Clare before his gaze came to a screeching halt on Hayley. She felt her stomach do a back flip as he caught and held her involuntary and fascinated regard. Scraping the last remnants of ice cream from the container, Jace gave Hayley his undivided attention while he concentrated on licking the spoon. His tongue was doing wonderfully wicked things to that inanimate and unappreciative piece of metal. Things that caused a flash of heat to course through her veins.

A melting sensation started in her belly and flowed down like hot wax. The result was an instant dampening of her panties. While the moisture in her body rushed south, the fire in her veins charged north. Hayley felt the warm wave radiate from her chest, throat and cheeks. Jace gave the spoon one last sensual lick before he smiled. It was a slow, wicked, teasing smile, as if he knew what effect he was having on her and was very, very pleased by it.

Irritated and mortified by how easily Jace got a reaction from her, Hayley instantly took affront. The man was far too sure of himself. Hayley was determined to prove she was no swooning virgin. She straightened her spine, lifted her chin and gave him a glare, uncaring of Bryn and Clare's intrigued looks.

Jace gave her an unrepentant grin and turned his attention back to Bryn. "Hope you don't mind," he said, indicating the empty carton. "It's my fee."

"Fee for what?" Bryn asked with a confused smile.

"Logan mentioned you had a cracked window in the living room. I volunteered to replace it." He disposed of the carton and rinsed the spoon. "Hello, Clare, nice to see you again."

"Jace," she acknowledged. "How goes the architectural business? Or should I not ask, since you're reduced to replacing broken windows for ice cream?"

"I just like to keep my hand in on the basics every now and then." He smiled. "The business is doing just fine. You know Gracie Stevens?"

Clare nodded.

"She just got a nice, fat settlement check from her old man. Seems she had a suspicion he was cheating on her and hired a private detective to catch him in the act. When she filed for divorce, a picture *was* worth a thousand words. And a hell of a lot of cash. She's looking to have some renovations done on that outdated mausoleum she's living in. It's gonna be a *sweet* job."

"Hmm, is it just the house she's looking to have renovated, or does she have some more *personal* adjustments in mind?" Clare asked with a teasing smile. She was well acquainted with Jace's reputation. He was a favorite among the local and not-so-local ladies.

"Some of both, I imagine," Jace answered, giving her a wicked wink.

Bryn cleared her throat. "Now I'm not so sure I want to introduce you to my sister."

Hayley, who'd watched the exchange between Clare and Jace with unwilling interest, found herself disgruntled by the talk of his exploits with women. The irritation she'd been feeling turned inward. *Why the hell should I care what he does?* she asked herself before speaking aloud. "Don't be silly, Bryn." Her tone of voice was cutting and cool. "If Mr. McKenna chooses to indulge in affairs with his clients, that's entirely his

21

business." She held out her hand. "Hayley Royden, pleased to meet you."

Jace transferred his blue-green gaze and open smile to Hayley, taking her hand. She'd had men undress her with their eyes before, but the way Jace looked at her now, she could almost believe that this man had actually *seen* her naked. She was puzzled by the unexplained recognition and heat that filled his eyes. It sent goose bumps marching over her skin. A sudden image of Jace naked was presented for her inspection by her all-too-vivid imagination. With an effort, Haley held on to her composure, keeping her expression neutral.

"Call me Jace. May I call you Hayley?" At her nod, he applied a gentle massaging pressure to her hand. "What you have to keep in mind, Hayley, is that a man doesn't always *accept* what he's offered. Just as I'm sure you yourself don't." His voice carried a gentle admonishment.

Haley bristled. "You are so right, Jace," she agreed pleasantly as she deliberately withdrew her hand from his. "There are some things a woman just couldn't tolerate," she added glacially.

Despite her irritation, Hayley couldn't deny the electric charge that caused her skin to tingle where his hand had touched hers. The heat flowing from his fingertips had swept in a wave up her arm and through her body, sending her temperature up a few notches. The sensation was reminiscent of submerging oneself in a warm and welcoming tub of water.

"It's always been my experience that a person can learn to tolerate quite a lot," Jace asserted in a husky growl as he stepped closer. "Even enjoy something they initially thought to dislike."

His eyes took on a hooded, sensual look that had no doubt seduced many an unwary woman. Hayley was not so easily taken in, and she stepped back, distancing herself while taking in a deep, calming breath. That turned out to be a mistake.

Softly subtle, Jace's scent invaded her nostrils. Warm, male musk beckoned and invited, while her arousal, swift and insistent, suddenly increased. Her insides tightened and she fought to still her quickening breath as her temperature rose yet another notch. It didn't help when she noticed a distinct thickening of the bulge that filled the space behind the zipper of his jeans. Hayley felt her mouth go dry as her pussy grew wetter.

"Perhaps some of us aren't that flexible," she managed to say, ungluing her tongue from the roof of her mouth.

"Oh well, flexibility. That's something that can always be worked on."

Jace's voice had taken on a warm, inviting timbre that drifted over her skin and stroked her nerve endings. She could well imagine some of the things he'd do to improve a woman's flexibility. Squelching the provocative images that flooded her mind, she narrowed her eyes and steeled her backbone. She was determined not to fall prey to this dangerously seductive man. Jace was clearly a man used to making easy conquests.

"Yes, that's true, but in order to achieve a goal, one must *want* it. If it's something you don't want, what's the point?"

"Sometimes a person isn't always sure of what they want, and it takes someone else to point them toward an experience that could very well change their entire life," Jace insisted.

"And what if that person is perfectly satisfied with their life?"

"Oh, Hayley," Jace shook his head with mock sadness. "While I believe there's perfect satisfaction to be had in some things," the look he gave her was scorching in its intensity, "I believe there's always room for change in a person's life. There's nothing like shaking things up and trying something new. Wouldn't you agree?"

Hayley felt herself relax, a reluctant smile tugging at her lips. Her irritation was quickly becoming amusement. Jace was obviously a man used to easily making sexual conquests, but he had a brain and wit to go with those devastating looks. Their banter was not only sexually stimulating, it was fun.

She raised an imperious brow and gave him a considering look. "While I agree there's nothing wrong with trying something new, that doesn't automatically mean it will be good for you. This new thing could turn out to be very, very bad."

"And yet some people find *bad* to be stimulating."

"That's true. Being reckless and wild certainly has its appeal, but often people regret being reckless when cooler heads prevail."

"I've found there are certain things over which intellect should have no sway. Sometimes it's better to act on instinct."

"And what if your instincts tell you to run before it's too late?"

"Running could actually be a good thing. There's nothing like the thrill of the chase."

Hayley had opened her mouth to reply when Clare burst out laughing. She turned to find Clare and Bryn watching the clearly flirtatious exchange. Bryn was staring at the two of them in wide-eyed astonishment.

"This was worth the loss of the butter pecan ice cream," Clare chortled. "Maybe you two should call it a draw."

Hayley gazed at Jace, noting the twinkle that lit his eyes. "I will if he will," she volunteered.

Jace inclined his head in agreement. "Fine by me, especially as I had the upper hand."

"You wish," Hayley snorted.

"Oh, honey, I don't need to *wish*."

"You just—"

"Stop!" Bryn yelled. "You're making me dizzy. Jace, are you done with the window?" He nodded. "Good, thank you for the repair, it was nice seeing you. Go home. Hayley, if you say one more word, you're grounded!"

24

Her words of protest were cut short as Bryn's cell phone rang. "Hello?" Bryn answered, keeping a vigilant eye on Hayley and Jace as Clare stood to the side snickering. "Hi, sweetheart. No, everything's fine. We're at the house, my house. I wanted to pick up some more of my things and Hayley wanted to see the place. Oh I've got some great news! Hayley's decided to move here, she's going to rent the house."

Hayley watched a slow, predatory smile curve Jace's lips as his eyes took on an intense, feral glow. A thrill of uncertainty tightened her stomach and she frowned, wondering if her eyes were playing tricks on her. The glow in Jace's eyes had been there then gone so fast that she wasn't sure she'd really seen it. She reluctantly concluded that it must have been a reflection of the light coming in the window. Yet she was left with a sensation of unease. Glow or not, there was still that all-too-satisfied smile to contend with.

He didn't give her the chance to tell him not to get any ideas. Without a word he turned and walked through to the living room to retrieve his tool box. She surreptitiously watched him go. *Damn, the man can move,* she thought, then muffled a groan as he bent to gather up his scattered tools. The sight of that firm little butt encased in tight jeans made Hayley's mouth water. She reluctantly pulled her attention back to Bryn's conversation with Logan.

"By the way, Jace is here. He fixed the window. It was really sweet of you to think of it." She listened for a moment and Hayley smiled as she watched a rosy blush heat her sister's cheeks. "Oh well...I'll think about that," Bryn answered with a slight purr in her voice. "Yes, he's right here. Okay. Jace? Logan wants to speak with you."

Jace took the phone Bryn handed him and retreated back into the living room. While he spoke with Logan, Bryn faced off with Hayley.

"What is *wrong* with you?" Bryn asked.

"What? It's not *me*, it's him!"

25

"You started it. And just for the record, I think you'd better steer clear of Jace. He's not exactly the boy next door."

"I'm no blushing virgin, Bryn. I can take care of myself."

"Even if you were, I'm sure Jace would be happy to help you with that," Clare quipped. "Did you see the way he looked at you? I felt the heat radiate all the way over here," she said, fanning herself.

Hayley grinned—leave it to Clare to go right to the more salient points of a situation. "Well, he can save his heat," she assured them. "I'm at just the right temperature."

"I'll agree with that," Jace interjected. "*Hot.*" He handed the phone back to Bryn, who said her goodbyes to Logan.

Jace's eyes locked with Hayley's. They smoldered with a muted blue-green fire, a banked, subtle glow that promised to become a raging inferno given the right fodder. Another heated flush ran the length of her body and Hayley made herself stand perfectly still, giving nothing away.

Jace turned his attention to Bryn. "Logan asked me to do a thorough run-through of the house. Since your sister's going to be staying here, he wants the whole place in good shape. He said for you to let me know if there's anything in particular you want done, or anything there's a problem with," he told her. "If it's all right with you, I'll keep the key Logan gave me. I'll bring some of my guys over tomorrow and we'll get started."

"That's sounds great, Jace. We'll be back tomorrow so I can clear out the rest of my things. I'll have a list ready of anything I think you should take a look at."

"Sounds good," he answered and, picking up his tool box, he headed for the door. "Ladies, it was a pleasure, as always." He sent Hayley an intense look that spoke volumes. "I'll see you tomorrow, Hayley."

"Well, won't that just be my lucky day," she returned sarcastically.

26

While Jace's appeal was undeniable, at this point she was certain getting involved with him would likely be more than dangerous. Jace was a heartbreak waiting to happen.

Jace laughed and sauntered out the door.

Hayley watched him go, a frown marring her face. Something about those wicked eyes of his seemed awfully familiar.

Chapter Two

ಬಿ

Bryn pulled up to her house and exited the car, list in hand. Jace's truck was already parked in the drive and she could see movement through the living room windows. She climbed the front steps and walked in the open front door. Jace was talking with two of his men, taking their reports about various aspects of the house's condition.

Seeing her enter, he gave her a smile and sent his guys about their business. "Hey, Bryn, good, you've got a list for me." He sent a searching look toward the open doorway. "I see Hayley decided retreat was the better part of valor. For now."

Bryn chuckled. "She said you gave her a headache. Well, actually, she said you were a pain in the ass and she was staying home to get some work done."

Jace's easy grin appeared. "I do like your little sis. She tells it like it is."

Bryn's smile faded. "Jace, Hayley's an adult and she'll do what she wants, but I can't help butting in, she is my sister, after all. Don't play games with her."

"I'm not playing, Bryn. She's *mine*."

A quiver shot through Bryn's stomach. "Are you sure?" she asked incredulously.

"Was Logan sure about you?"

"I guess that was a stupid question." She frowned and bit her lip. "Oh dear, this is…this is…really unexpected. Have you told Logan?"

Jace shook his head. "You're the first, and you have my permission to tell him. I'm going to discuss it with Cade. As my beta he has the right to be informed, but no one else is to know until it's a done deal."

Bryn nodded. "Jace, you know this isn't going to be easy. It was one thing for Logan to choose a human mate, although I guess *choose* isn't the right word since it's not really a choice, it just *is*. But the point is—he isn't head of a pack. *You*, on the other hand, are Iron Tower's alpha. I can't see everyone happily accepting Hayley as their alpha female, especially some of the women. There are some who make no secret of the fact that they expect to win that position."

"Don't think I haven't thought about all the problems, Bryn, but as you said, this is not really a choice. It just *is*. Hayley is my mate. I recognized that fact when I first caught her scent. This is not some political appointment, it's a choice ruled by the physical and emotional. Any expectations that members of my pack have will be dealt with. From what I can see, Hayley's no coward and she's strong-willed. I just have to show her my sterling qualities and convince her I'm the man of her dreams. I have no doubt she can handle the rest." A wry twinkle lit Jace's eyes.

"This should be fun," Bryn laughed. "You two got off to such a *great* start yesterday."

"Actually, I think we *did* get off to a great start. In relationships that start with conflict, the conflict is the subconscious reaction of the two involved to fight their inner wants and needs."

"I didn't know you were a junior psychologist."

"I have many talents," Jace replied with a wicked wink.

Bryn sighed and rolled her eyes. "My poor sister." She caught and held Jace's regard, her gaze suddenly deadly serious. "You know if you hurt her, you'll have to contend not only with Logan but with me, don't you?"

Jace reached for her hand and brought it to his cheek, rubbing it against his skin before kissing her knuckles. "If I hurt her, you have my permission to kick my ass, but Bryn, it's not going to happen. I promise you, I'll take care of her. I'm...I'm not..."

She reached up and stroked his cheek. "You're not just the free and easy bachelor image you project. You're a good man, Jace, strong, reliable, protective." She smiled, her eyes glistening. "You have my approval to court my sister, and may you both enjoy the chase...brother."

His grin lit the room. "Thanks, sis. By the way, did I mention you need a new roof?"

"*What?*"

"Lucky for you, I only charge family the cost of materials."

* * * * *

Thighs spread wide, she arched her back under the sensual strokes of the clever tongue that explored her quivering pussy. Sweat dotted her skin and the gentle breeze from the ceiling fan tightened her nipples. She reached up to pluck at one tight kernel and groaned as a large hand slid the length of her body and cupped her other breast, its fingers echoing her own movements.

She groaned again and struggled under him as he gently sucked her clit, his tongue stroking slowly over the sensitized bud. "Oh fuck! James, James, please," she pleaded. "Fuck me, Jace!"

"Jace?" Hayley exclaimed as she quickly hit the backspace button and added the correct name. Relieved to have the evidence of her slip erased, she sighed, stretched and turned off her laptop. She was pleased at having gotten quite a bit done on her latest book, despite her tendency to be distracted by thoughts of Jace. Submerging herself in the lives of her characters helped her to put reality out of her head for a time, but the trouble with reality was that it always reasserted itself.

She was ready to admit that Jace McKenna had made a definite impression on her. She was fascinated by his bad-boy image and her body reacted in a way she couldn't deny. She wanted him. Hayley squirmed in her chair. Writing sex scenes always got her motor revved, but putting herself and Jace in the picture made her ache.

"Damn," she whispered. "I want more than that!"

The feeling was so intense, her chest tightened and tears glittered in her eyes. She swept a hand through her hair then propped it under her chin and stared out the window. *This sucks*, she thought. *He's definitely not the kind of guy who's looking for a wife, children and stability… I sure know how to pick 'em.*

Hayley sat and brooded for a while, unable to come up with any answers to her dilemma. The rumbling complaint of her stomach pulled her from her thoughts. She decided to go downstairs in search of some lunch. She found Logan there ahead of her.

"Hey, bro, what's cookin'?" she teased.

"You're just in time, li'l sis," he shot back with a grin. "Bryn's on her way home with barbequed ribs and I'm fixing a salad to go with them. Do me a favor and slide that loaf of bread in the oven."

Hayley complied then sat at the island and watched Logan as he efficiently put together the salad. "Logan…" she began then stopped, not sure how to continue.

"What's on your mind, Hayley?"

"Jace McKenna," she blurted out then fidgeted in her chair as a blush suffused her cheeks.

"I see… Bryn said you met yesterday."

"Yeah."

"You like him?"

"I don't know if that's the word for it. I'm not sure how I feel. I just know he stirred something up inside me and I'm not sure what to do about it."

Logan smiled and washed his hands before taking a seat next to her. "Let me tell you a little about Jace. His dad died when he was eleven. His mother took it very hard and Jace had to grow up faster than any kid that age should. He struggled to become the man of the family. He succeeded. He took care of his mother and sisters. He stayed focused and serious."

Hayley nodded, fascinated with this unexpected view of Jace.

"When he turned nineteen, his mother met a man, fell in love and remarried. She and the girls moved two states over to be with him. Jace decided he wanted to stay here. For the first time in eight years, he didn't have to be responsible for anyone but himself. I don't think I have to go into too much detail when I say that as a young, free male, Jace had his share of good times."

Hayley shook her head and gave him a rueful smile.

"He made up for those lost years of his youth in spades, but at the same time, he studied hard and made something of himself. He's a successful and sought after architect who knows the value of responsibility and reliability. Yes, he's got a wild streak, but when Jace wants something he goes after it, he takes care of it, he even nurtures it."

"It's hard to believe that all that's under the surface. He just seems like a typical bad boy out for a good time."

Logan smiled. "I know. I'm afraid that's a typical male persona. We like to pretend we're just out for fun and don't need any stability in our lives. But I gotta tell you, Hayley, that kind of life's way overrated."

"So speaks the voice of experience?"

"Oh yeah. You have no idea how glad I was to find Bryn. She's changed my life in ways I only imagined. I couldn't be happier."

"You think Jace might be looking for the same thing?"

"He'd never admit it, but yes, he is."

"That's good to know, but I'm still...well...afraid to make any kind of move. I mean what if I get serious and he doesn't?"

Logan grinned. "Well now, you see, that's where you have an advantage."

Hayley frowned. "I don't get it."

"Jace knows that if he fools around and hurts you, he's going to have to answer to Bryn and me. If you let him know you're interested and he doesn't feel anything for you, he'll avoid you in order to avoid a conflict with us. But if he feels there's something special between you, nothing is going to keep him away."

Understanding dawned in Hayley's eyes and she chuckled. "This could turn out to be fun."

Logan raised a brow. "Why do I get the feeling my best friend is in for a big load of trouble?"

"Now, Logan," Hayley teased. "Would I cause your friend trouble?"

He looked her over, noting the devilish gleam in her eyes. "Oh yeah, he's in trouble."

The two of them burst out laughing just as Bryn walked in the kitchen door. "All right, what did I miss?"

Chapter Three

ຂວ

The weather had been marred by rain, but a few days later it dawned bright and sunny. Hayley was anticipating her next encounter with Jace. She knew from Bryn that he would be at the house working on the new roof and she planned to begin moving her things in, as the interior problems were already taken care of.

Bryn and Logan had sincerely urged her to stay, but she wanted to give them their privacy, imagining how she'd feel if she had to host her sister when beginning a new life with the man she loved. Something like that would have a tendency to take the edge off the spontaneity of the romance. There'd be no impromptu lovemaking in front of the fireplace or on the kitchen table if your sister might walk in at any moment.

What a bummer, she thought with a grin.

After breakfast, she spent some time loading her car with the boxes her parents had sent her after she'd phoned them telling them about her decision to move to Whispering Springs. Like Bryn, they had reservations about her quitting her job, but as usual, they offered their support. They were actually pleased that their daughters were together in one place where they would be able to look after each other.

Having saved her precious laptop for last, Hayley picked the case up and made her final trip downstairs. Logan and Bryn were gone for the day. She locked the door behind her and carefully settled the case in the passenger seat of her car before she took her place behind the wheel.

Hayley took the drive to the house at a slow, relaxed pace, admiring the view and letting her anticipation build. After her talk with Logan, she was on pins and needles wondering what Jace's next move might be or even if he would make one. She hated the idea that he might not feel anything but lust for her and conceded the fact that she might be in for a big disappointment. Ultimately, she was glad that one way or another, in the next few minutes she'd know for sure.

As she approached the house, the sight of Jace's truck in the driveway made her stomach tighten. She ordered herself to calm down and parked her car beside his truck. The first thing she noticed was the sound of pounding, but no one was in sight. Taking her laptop with her, she walked up the steps and across the porch. Using her key, she let herself in the front entryway.

Hayley set her case on the sofa and walked through the kitchen and out the open back door. Following the rhythmic sounds of hammering, she made her way down the back steps and out into the yard, turning to look up on the roof. Perched above her, hard at work and seemingly unconcerned with the height, Jace was pounding a roofing nail into a shingle panel.

Hayley's heart fluttered and her mouth dropped open. In deference to the heat, Jace had removed his shirt. His torso gleamed with a light sheen of sweat, the muscles in his back flexed with every move and when he adjusted his position, turning slightly, she could see the sculpted plains, ridges and valleys of his chest. His upper chest was covered with a dark mat of hair that made Hayley's fingers twitch with the need to touch.

For her, the only thing as blatantly male as a muscular chest covered with hair was a thick, hard cock. *Oh that is so not fair,* she thought, automatically conceding the first round to Jace in a competition he wasn't even aware he was in. With an effort, she snapped her jaw closed, took a deep breath then spoke to get his attention.

"Hey," she called out.

Jace turned his head and smiled when he saw her. "Hey, yourself. Beautiful day, isn't it?"

"Oh yeah," she replied with feeling.

Jace grinned as though knowing the reason for her vehemence. "You all set to move in?"

"Yes, I brought some boxes my parents sent and I have a couple of suitcases."

"Wait a sec and I'll give you a hand hauling them in."

Unable to deny the enjoyment she was receiving from watching him, Hayley waited patiently as he placed a couple more nails, hammered them in then easily made his way across the slanting roof to the ladder that awaited him. Jace clambered down without hesitation and she had to admire his sure and steady movements.

As soon as his feet hit the ground, he walked toward her. An involuntary shiver slid through her. Jace walked like a graceful predator on the hunt and Hayley suddenly felt like the prey. She stood mesmerized until he halted in front of her.

His gaze bore into hers and he reached out, hooking a finger under her chin while gently pushing up. "Better close this, sweetheart. You never know what might take a notion to slide between those luscious lips of yours."

Hayley blushed furiously and snapped her mouth shut with an audible click.

Jace smiled, his eyes twinkling with amusement. "So where are those boxes?"

Hayley turned and walked back into the house. "In the trunk of my car, I can get them."

"No problem, I'm here to help. With *anything* you need."

Keeping her back to him, Hayley rolled her eyes and silently berated herself. She was definitely losing ground fast. Jace's sexy and unabashed display had turned her into a walking cream puff with jelly-filled knees. Marshalling her defenses, she decided it was time to turn the tables.

As she led the way to the car, she could feel his silent perusal of her backside. Just to even things out, she put a little extra sway in her hips. She smiled her own amused smile at the deep intake of breath that sounded behind her. Apparently, she wasn't the only one who enjoyed a nice view.

Reaching the car, she sternly suppressed her smile and opened the trunk. As she moved back out of the way, Jace reached in to grab the first box, his arm accidentally brushing the side of her breast. Hayley's breath immediately seized as a zing of lightning shot through her.

"Sorry," he apologized tersely and picked up the box, carrying it into the house.

"S'all right," she acknowledged weakly and leaned against the car for a moment to catch her breath. "If he ever touches me with any kind of intent, I'll probably pass out," she mumbled with disgust before opening the back door of the car to drag out one of her suitcases.

They passed each other several times as they made trips into the house with her things, until the car was finally unloaded. Each time Jace approached, Hayley was so hyperaware of him, her muscles tensed until she felt like she was walking in a mine field, waiting for the first explosion. She sighed with relief when the job was done and noticed Jace rubbing the back of his neck. Suddenly she realized that she wasn't the only one feeling the tension. That made her feel much better and she managed to relax a bit as she followed him into the kitchen.

With easy familiarity, Jace opened one of the kitchen cupboards and took out a glass. "Do you mind? I'm really thirsty."

"Of course I don't mind. You need to stay hydrated while you're working out in the sun. Are you wearing any sunblock?"

Turning with his full glass of water in hand, Jace brought the rim to his lips and drank. Crystal clear droplets of water fell from the glass and landed on his chest. Hayley watched in rapt fascination as they took a slow meandering path through the forest of silky black hair. One bold drop slid over his rounded pectoral muscle and headed straight for his nipple. It balanced on the tip in a sparkling, teasing dance before dropping down to land on the jean-clad thigh of one slightly cocked leg.

"Oh fuck," she breathed, then coughed noisily to cover her slip.

"You okay?" Jace asked with concern. "You look like you could use some water yourself."

He refilled the glass and handed it to her. Hayley downed the contents in record time while Jace looked on with a raised brow. He absently reached up to rub the damp patches on his chest that were left behind by the errant water drops. When the tiny brown nubs of his nipples tightened under his touch, Hayley's last swallow of water went the wrong way. She began to cough in earnest.

"Take it easy, darlin', there's lots more water where that came from," he teased as he gently patted her back. "No need to be in such a hurry. Most things are better when they're taken slow."

Hayley gave a final wheeze and peered at him through watering eyes. The man was an expert at delivering innuendos while managing to look perfectly innocent.

"I was thirsty," she defended lamely.

"I see that. I'll be back in a minute. I'd like you to do something for me, if you will."

Fortunately for her, she couldn't see the delighted grin that wreathed Jace's face as he walked away.

With careful deliberation she set the empty glass on the counter and shook her head in disgust. *Hayley Royden, what the hell's wrong with you? He's actually interested and you're turning into some kind of a clown! Now get a hold of yourself before he gets the idea you're a total idiot and backs off!*

Seeing Jace through the window as he returned with a bottle in his hand, she straightened from her slouch against the counter. He walked in the door and held up the bottle.

"Sunblock, thanks for reminding me. I put some on earlier, but I had a hard time reaching my back. I'm sure I probably missed some spots, so…would you mind?" he asked innocently, handing her the bottle and turning his back to her.

Hayley stared at the wide expanse of masculine flesh before her, scrunched her face in a quick grimace and took a deep breath. *I can do this, I can do this,* she thought while out loud she replied, "Sure, happy to help."

She opened the bottle and poured a generous dollop of the white cream into her hand, set the bottle down, then rubbed it between her palms, warming it before applying it to Jace's back. He let out a small "mmm" of pleasure as her hands began massaging the lotion into his skin.

His skin was every bit as warm and smooth as it looked. The muscles in his back were firm and her fingers easily traced the delineated bundles as her hands glided over him. Hayley breathed deeply and lost herself in the rhythm of her massage. Instead of being uncomfortable, touching Jace seemed to be the most natural thing in the world. An easy and open connection formed between them, until they were both swaying to the beat of her stroking hands. Her hands moved to his shoulders and she kneaded the muscles there until Jace's husky groan of pleasure broke the spell that wove them together.

Hayley stepped back. "There, I think that covers it," she said breathlessly and took another step to the sink to wash her hands.

She could feel Jace watching her and knew the moment he moved. From beside her his voice spoke softly. "Thanks, Hayley, you've got a nice touch, darlin'. You know, I get this pain in my back now and then, do you think you might consider…"

Hayley turned, a smile on her lips. "Go back to work, Jace."

"Well now, that's just cruel." He chuckled and walked out the door.

Hayley continued to smile as she watched him go. Her eyes narrowed as a plan formed. Jace had definitely come out the winner in this round, but the fight had just begun. "Time for round two," she murmured and went to the bedroom to change.

* * * * *

Jace was back on the roof and giving free rein to a grin that wouldn't be repressed. Hayley was his and she was unmistakably responding to him. *The old McKenna charm is right on track,* he thought smugly as he returned to placing shingles on the roof and nailing them down.

He replayed their encounter with satisfaction. He'd been smooth and confident while Hayley was definitely off balance, just where he wanted her. His own composure had taken a hit when he'd accidentally touched her breast while helping with the boxes in the trunk of her car. She wasn't the only one who'd been affected by that incident, but he'd recovered quickly.

The longer he was in contact with her, the deeper he felt the primal need building inside of him. Its source was directly centered in the place that sheltered his wolf, and his instincts fed the need. It was only his strength of will that kept him from telling Hayley just what he wanted and who she was to him. But he knew it was too soon and he wasn't about to chance messing this up. The more smoothly he could make things go, the sooner Hayley would undeniably be his.

Catching a movement out of the corner of his eye, he looked down to find Hayley walking out onto the lawn. Barefoot, she was carrying a large towel over one arm and she'd changed her clothes. Jace's eyes widened in appreciation.

She was wearing an extremely short pair of cutoffs. From the back, all he could see of her top was a string running across her bare back and one that ended in a tie at the back of her neck. As he watched, she stopped, shook out the towel and bent over to lay it on the ground.

When her shorts rode up to reveal the smooth creamy flesh of her bottom, two things happened. First, Jace's heart rate increased, the newly racing blood that pounded in his veins headed straight for his cock, then his aim suddenly went awry. The next stroke of the hammer found his thumb instead of the nail he'd been aiming at, and the blood that had filled his cock suddenly ran back where it had come from.

"Son of a bitch!" he yelled as he stood and shook the abused digit before cradling it in his other hand.

Hayley spun around and Jace got his second surprise. The top she wore, if it could be called that, barely covered her. The cherry-red fabric was centered over her lush breasts. It cradled that generously firm flesh, hiding her nipples while leaving much of the upper portion of her breasts exposed.

"Son of a *bitch*," he groaned with feeling, and became dizzy when his blood again reversed direction, draining from his head and filling his cock. He lost his footing.

Hayley screamed as Jace scrambled to regain his balance. Barely making it, he ended up sitting down hard on the roof.

"Are you all right?" she yelled, clearly concerned.

Jace rolled his eyes, thoroughly disgusted with himself. "I'm fine, just fine," he ground out through gritted teeth.

"That's good. I really thought you were going to fall. You shouldn't fool around like that, you know."

"That's fine advice, I'll be sure to follow that from now on."

"Now don't get snippy. It's not my fault you're a klutz."

"I am *not* a klutz!"

41

"Whatever. I'm going to get some sun, if you don't mind."

"Why should I mind?"

"No reason. Since your work has sort of been interrupted already, would you mind coming down and putting some of this lotion on my back?"

Jace gave her a long, silent stare. "Don't tempt me, Hayley. That can be a dangerous game to play."

"What do you mean?"

"If I come down there and put my hands on you, I'm not going to stop at spreading lotion on your back. That skimpy little top you're *almost* wearing will be the first thing to go," he informed her as embers began to smolder in his eyes. "Then those little shorts are gone and if you're wearing panties, you won't be for long," he promised. "*Then* I'll start with the lotion. The first place my hands go will be on that sweet ass of yours, then up your back and around to the front."

Hayley stood in shocked silence, her body electrified by every word Jace uttered.

"I can't wait to hold your breasts in my hands. They're beautiful, Hayley—a real treasure—and I'll show you just how much I appreciate them. I'm going to make you feel so good when I lick and suck your nipples."

Said nipples reacted as an involuntary shiver rippled over her skin. They tightened and pushed impudently against the fabric that hid them.

Jace growled—there was no other word to describe the sound that rumbled from his chest. "That's right, sweetheart, just think about how good it's going to feel when I taste you."

"Jace, stop," she murmured halfheartedly. Her breathing had turned into a ragged pant.

"While I'm suckling you, my hands will be free and they're going to head straight for your hot, wet little pussy—and you *will* be wet, Hayley. You're wet right now, aren't you?"

"That's enough!" she yelled as a wave of dizziness swept over her.

"Between the lotion and your sweet, hot juices, I'll be able to slide a couple of fingers right in."

"Stop already! You win. Okay? You win! I'm going in the house, you smart-mouthed, ultra-competitive bastard." Hayley stomped away in a snit.

Jace smiled and murmured to himself, "Never tempt a wolf, darlin'."

He stood, grimaced at his sore thumb and rubbed his abused posterior, deciding that, all things considered, the look on Hayley's face had been worth the pain. With a jaunty whistle he went back to work.

In the house, Hayley marched to her bedroom, fell back on the bed and lay there giggling.

"*Oh yeah*, he wants me."

Chapter Four

ജ

A couple of days later, Hayley was sitting at her computer when the phone rang. She picked it up but before she could say anything a voice said, "Ready to have some fun?"

She smiled at the sound of her sister's voice. "Now, Bryn, you know I'm not into threesomes," she teased.

"You should be so lucky, sister mine," Bryn replied with a snort. "Logan's invited us out. If you're interested, we're going to meet at Morgan's. It's a local tavern, nice place, really. The owner doesn't allow any rowdy stuff. What do you think?"

"Sounds like fun. I could use a night out."

"That's what I figured. You've been pretty hard at it, haven't you?"

"I've got to get myself established, Bryn. I really want to make a success of this."

"You know, it's good to see you so intense about something. I've always had the impression that you were never really happy with any job you've held."

"You got that right. Most times, the only reason I hung on to a job was because that's where the money was coming from. It's not a very satisfying reason to work. But writing? It's fun, Bryn. It's fulfilling something inside me that I didn't even know I needed."

"I'm really happy for you, Hayley. Now, all seriousness aside, I'll pick you up at six forty-five. Logan's supposed to meet us there at seven."

"I'll be ready. What's the dress code?"

"Strictly casual. Jeans are par for the course."

"That's easy. See you in a little while."

"Bye."

Hayley hung up the phone and went to her bedroom to dig out her favorite pair of jeans, which she paired with a red cotton tank top. After taking a quick shower and blow-drying her hair, she slipped into a lacy red bra and panties set. She applied her makeup with a light hand, a little foundation and a wisp of mascara. Once dressed, she tucked her driver's license, some cash, a comb, house key and lip gloss into her pockets.

She slipped her feet into a pair of sandals and was just reaching for a deep red suede shirt, in case it should turn cooler, when she heard the sound of Bryn's horn in the driveway.

"Right on time," she commented with a smile and headed for the front door. Stepping out, she made sure it locked tight and joined her sister in the car.

The ride was short and they arrived ten minutes later. Morgan's was located at the edge of town. It was flanked on one side by a twenty-four-hour convenience store-gas station and a bowling alley on the other. Early as it was, the parking lot was fairly full. Morgan's was a popular place, especially— unbeknownst to Hayley—with the two local werewolf packs. David Morgan, the owner, was a member of Iron Tower pack and ran his place very diplomatically. There was no trouble allowed, anyone breaking the rules was summarily ejected and never allowed to return. Not wanting to lose their privileges, most of the patrons went out of their way to keep the peace.

The two sisters drew many an admiring gaze when they walked in the door. The locals were familiar with Bryn and knew that she was Logan Sutherland's mate and part-owner of the Whispering Springs Bookstore. And small-town gossip had already ensured that word got around of her sister Hayley's arrival.

David caught sight of them from behind the bar and walked around to greet them with a welcoming smile. "Bryn, it's good to see you. Logan coming?"

"Yes, he should be here any minute now. David, I'd like you to meet my sister, Hayley. Hayley, this is David Morgan. He owns this fine establishment."

David grinned. "Pleased to meet you, Hayley."

"Same here," she answered with a smile.

"You ladies follow me. I've got an empty booth waiting for you."

David led the way to a large booth and after they were seated, took their drink orders.

"Just cola for me," Bryn told him while Hayley ordered a light beer.

Hayley admired the place, her foot tapping in time to the music that filled the room in a modified blare. It was spacious, the booths and tables large and well-spaced so as not to crowd the patrons. There was even a small dance floor in front of the jukebox for those inclined toward a little exercise. The whole place was reminiscent of a large rustic cabin. At the back, there was a quarter loft that was reached by stairs on either side of the room. It was set with tables for those who wanted a bird's-eye view of the ground floor or just a bit more privacy.

In her mind's eye, Hayley could picture this as a scene set in Alaska during the gold rush. The place would be filled with saloon girls and crusty miners out spending their gold while looking for a good time. She smiled and sipped her beer.

"You like it?" Bryn asked.

"Very nice," she answered. "I was just thinking it would make a great background for a scene in a book."

"I could see it," Bryn agreed.

They continued to chat and sip their drinks as the minutes ticked by. Bryn looked at her watch. "He's late, I hope everything's all right."

"I'm sure it is. Don't fuss, sis, he'll be here."

A few moments later a shadow fell across the table. They both looked up, expecting to see Logan, but instead found a stranger standing there. The man was tall and heavily built, his features coarse under a raspy growth of beard. Hayley was sure he probably thought it was sexy. There was an expectant arrogance in his eyes she took immediate umbrage to. That, and the fact that his clothes were unkempt and his odor indicated a lack of personal hygiene.

He directed his gaze to Bryn. "Hey there, little lady, how about a dance?"

"No, thank you," Bryn answered frostily. "I'm waiting for my fiancé."

"Oooh, your fiancé—well, la-dee-da. I'm sure he won't mind if you dance while you're waiting. Come on, I'll show you what it's like to be with a *real* man."

He reached out, intent on grabbing Bryn's arm. Hayley lashed out with lightning speed, grabbing his wrist as she rose from the booth and forced him back a step. "Don't touch my sister," she ordered. Her voice was deceptively calm, her gaze hard and direct. She released him and surreptitiously wiped her hand on the side of her thigh. "She told you she's waiting for someone. Why don't you go back to your table?"

"Well now, there's no need to be jealous. I got plenty for the two of you," he leered and grabbed his crotch, rubbing it obscenely. "How about I give you the first taste?"

Again he reached out, this time his hand zoning in on Hayley's breast. Without hesitation she grabbed his arm, stepped to the side and in a totally unexpected and graceful move, swept the offender's feet from under him and sent him crashing to the floor. On the way down, there was a loud rip as his hand caught in the armhole of her shirt and ripped the shoulder seam loose.

Hayley stood over the man. Even with her hair mussed, face flushed and half her bra visible through her ripped shirt, she was the very picture of an avenging Amazon. What she didn't know was that at the very moment she took the man down, the front door opened and Logan, accompanied by Jace, arrived just in time to see her in action.

For a split second, the entire room froze. The only sound was the continued wailing of the jukebox. As quickly as the room froze, it suddenly thawed and a buzz of conversation swept through the crowd. David Morgan arrived just as Logan and Jace pushed their way through the crowd.

"What the hell's going on here?" Jace demanded.

"This jackass made a pass at Bryn. When I politely asked him to leave, he tried to grab me," Hayley explained.

David glanced from Logan to Jace and saw twin storms brewing. "I'll take care of this," he told them as he saw the angry protests that were heading his way. He didn't give them a chance to object. "Out there, your word is law and I respect that. But this is my place, my rules, no exceptions. This asshole's not worth the trouble a private lesson in manners might bring. Sit. Take care of your ladies. All your drinks this evening are on the house."

He signaled two of his bartenders. They grabbed the man and frog-marched him out the door. Two other men rose from their table and followed their unfortunate friend out. Moments later, the sound of three motorcycles peeling away was heard from the parking lot.

"Bryn, Hayley, I'm sorry for the trouble—believe me, this is not the norm around here. Those three obviously didn't know the rules," David apologized.

"It's okay, David, it wasn't your fault. It all happened so fast. Fortunately my sister is some kind of ninja master," Bryn announced with a grin.

"Bull." Hayley blushed. She slid into the booth and sat back with a sigh then tensed slightly as Jace slid in beside her. Logan and Bryn took places across from them.

"You're bleeding," Jace commented quietly, his voice vibrating with suppressed anger and frustration.

Craning her neck, Hayley tried to see what he was talking about. "I can't see it," she complained.

"Here, lean this way."

Jace took up a napkin and dipped it in one of the glasses of water that had been delivered to their table along with fresh drinks for Bryn and Hayley and beers for himself and Logan. His hand cupped Hayley's shoulder and he lightly swabbed the angry scratch that marred the creamy flesh of her throat.

Hayley hissed at the contact and he gentled his touch, cleaning the scratch and patting it dry. He gently tucked the loose edge of her shirt under her bra strap, a move that caused her to shiver. "There, it's not bleeding anymore, but you'd better put some antibacterial salve on it when you get home. If you don't have some, I'll get some from the store next door—in fact, maybe I should do that now," he offered and made to rise.

"Jace, sit down. You're not going out to look for that guy," Logan ordered.

Jace kept quiet, his blue-green eyes stormy with protest as he struggled to get himself under control. "He touched her. He hurt her." Jace's words were staccato and thick with emotion.

"I know, but she's okay. Hayley, tell Jace you're okay," Logan's voice was pitched to soothe, the command softly spoken.

Hayley frowned and looked from Jace to Logan and back again. There was something going on, but she hadn't a clue what it was. Logan's gaze was filled with concern that she knew was directed at Jace. His expression clearly stated that she had to do something about it.

She turned her confused gaze to Bryn who nodded in encouragement. Shrugging, she turned in her seat to face him. "Jace, I'm okay. Really I am."

A small gasp escaped Hayley's lips as he returned her regard. Jace's eyes were glowing, there was no mistaking it. No sunlight or candlelight or lamplight could cause that inner fire. Fascinated, she leaned forward, her hand going up to cup his cheek. He immediately took her hand in his and turned it palm up to his nose, drawing deeply of her scent. Eyes closing in what looked like contented bliss, his tongue flicked out to slide sensuously over her palm.

Hayley shivered, her breath beginning to race. When Jace opened his eyes, the glow was gone. "You sure you're all right, baby?" he questioned softly, his voice caressing, enfolding her with warmth.

Dumbfounded, she could only nod, stunned by the intensity of Jace's concern for her.

Coiled tension drained from him. She could see his body take on a more relaxed stance. "Good."

He released her hand, picked up one of the beers and took several healthy swallows. "Now how about you tell me where you learned that little trick you used on that guy."

She blinked. Suddenly everything was back to normal. It was almost as though she'd taken a mini trip into another dimension and was suddenly returned to reality. No one commented on Jace's behavior or the unbelievable fact that his eyes had been glowing like Chinese lanterns. Logan and Bryn were looking on with complaisant approval, not in the least disconcerted by anything that had passed in the last few moments.

"I will if you tell me why your eyes were glowing a moment ago."

"Oh that," Jace smiled. "That's just something that happens when I get very emotional about something. It's a...well...it's a condition I have. I'll explain it in more detail someday, but not now, okay?"

Moved by the unexpected plea in his voice, she nodded her agreement.

"Your turn."

"Um, I took some classes in self-defense. Thought it might come in handy, you know?"

"It certainly came in handy tonight," Logan commented. "Thank you, Hayley, for looking after Bryn."

Hayley smiled sheepishly and shrugged. "She's my sister—we've always looked out for each other."

"Yes we have," Bryn said with a smile. "Remember when we were little and Johnny Tebbits tried to steal our lunch money? He was a big elementary school bully a grade ahead of me and two grades ahead of Hayley," she told the guys. "He thought he was going to have it easy, terrorizing a couple of girls." She giggled. "Hayley and I jumped on him. He never bothered us again!"

"Logan, I think we're sitting with a couple of bold, no-nonsense women. You'd better watch yourself, buddy."

"Oh I don't need to. Bryn's already got me where she wants me. I think you're the one who'd better watch out. Hayley just showed us how she handles a man who gets out of line."

Jace paused, a thoughtful and speculative look on his face. "That's true, but then I like wrestling matches."

"I don't wrestle, and in class we were told one of the best methods for subduing a recalcitrant male was to go straight for the gonads."

"Ouch." Jace squirmed in his seat. "I think I'll concede this round to you." He raised his glass in a salute while Logan and Bryn chuckled and Hayley gave him a satisfied smirk.

They spent the rest of the evening enjoying the atmosphere, drinks and conversation. When he wasn't playing man-on-the-make, Hayley found Jace to be quite intelligent. He was very knowledgeable about current events and stated his opinions with a well-thought-out thoroughness that proved there was more in his head than the measurements of the female body. In spite of the fact that the drinks were free, he limited himself to two beers, as did Logan. She had to admire them for that. Most guys would have taken advantage of such an opportunity for all it was worth.

"How about a dance?"

"Hmm?" Hayley replied, realizing she'd been lost in thought and not really paying attention to the conversation that continued around her.

"Dance?" Jace repeated.

"Oh, well..."

"Go on, Hayley. You love to dance," Bryn encouraged with a mischievous smile.

Hayley sent a moue and a narrow-eyed look her way. The thought of dancing with Jace, of having any kind of bodily contact with him, made her knees feel weak.

Jace slid from the booth and held out his hand to her. "Come on, darlin'. You're no coward."

Unable to think of a viable excuse, she took his hand, slid across the seat and let him lead her to the little dance floor in front of the jukebox. Several other couples already occupied the space, for which she was grateful. At least she wouldn't feel conspicuous being the only couple dancing. The selection on the jukebox chose that moment to change to a slow song with a rolling, sensual beat. Jace expertly took her in his arms and began to move.

Hayley automatically followed his movements, her body picking up his rhythm and aligning itself to his. She stared with mute fascination into his eyes, watching the vibrant blue-green take on the glow of a banked fire. With perfect clarity, his eyes reflected his emotions. In addition to his unmistakable arousal there was something else blossoming there, something that sent a wild hope surging through her and yet scared her at the same time. Unable to maintain eye contact with him, Hayley ducked her head and laid it on his shoulder. Jace sighed and pulled her closer until there wasn't a space to be found between them.

He buried his face in her hair and Hayley could feel his chest rise as he inhaled deeply. "You smell so damn good," he growled. "Makes me feel things. Never felt like this before." His voice was filled with wonder.

Hayley shivered at the husky rasp of his tone and burrowed closer, feeling the hard bulge of his unmistakable erection pressing into her belly. Far from being offended, she reveled in her power as a woman. Her own desires rose proportionately and Hayley welcomed them, knowing they were real and right and natural—her response to this man who was making a place for himself in her life.

They danced together in a world of their own, filled with heat and need, tempered by patience, longing and hope and the realization of something just beginning. As the music ended, they drew apart and smiled at each other. Each of them knew without asking that the other understood exactly what was happening. Jace placed a soft kiss on her cheek and led her back to their table.

Hayley took her seat and turned to Jace as he slid in beside her. "By the way, what are you doing here? No one told me you were coming."

Jace smiled. "I more or less invited myself when Logan told me he was meeting you and Bryn."

"I see," she answered. "Any particular reason why?"

"Are you fishin' for somethin', sweetheart?"

"Just curious."

"Uh-huh. Do I really need to spell out for you why I'm here?" Jace gave her a look that melted her insides like butter.

Hayley swallowed hard. "I think that look tells me everything I need to know."

Across the booth Logan snorted on a laugh and sent a wink Hayley's way, his expression clearly conveying an "I told you so". Hayley shrugged sheepishly but was pleased.

As the evening rolled to a close, Bryn began to yawn and Logan declared it was time to go. He was very solicitous of her, helping her up while putting an arm around her shoulders, pulling her close to his side. Hayley saw the liquid warmth that filled Bryn's eyes when she looked up at him, and sighed when Logan bent to place a soft kiss on Bryn's lips.

Jace had already risen and she slid out of the booth to find him watching her, a solemn expression in his eyes. He turned to Logan. "Why don't you take Bryn home in her car? I'll drop Hayley off, if that's okay with you?" he asked her.

Hayley nodded her acceptance, a single butterfly sending a slight flutter through her stomach. She wasn't really certain what to expect, but at the same time, she felt inexplicably safe with Jace.

As everyone agreed to the arrangements, they said their goodbyes in the parking lot. Jace led Hayley to his truck and opened the passenger door for her. She settled in and fastened her seatbelt as he rounded the front of the truck and took his place beside her.

Jace turned the radio on to some soft music, and despite the fact that there was no conversation during the drive, Hayley felt herself relax. She laid her head back on the leather-covered seat and briefly closed her eyes.

"Tired?" Jace asked softly as he pulled in her driveway.

"A little. It was an interesting evening."

"That it was," he agreed and shut the motor off while leaving the music to play. "How's the scratch?"

"It stings a bit."

"Let me see."

He leaned toward her and Hayley twisted her body around and leaned in toward him. His fingertips were gentle as they traced the outer edge of the scratch.

"It's been bleeding again. Let me take care of it," he breathed.

Not realizing what he intended, Hayley's breath caught in her throat as he nuzzled his mouth against her skin and his tongue made a long, wet and very slow path along the scratch. Her breath came in a series of quiet pants and she whimpered softly as he repeated the gesture again and again.

Jace pulled back slightly, his eyes gleaming with the now-familiar lambent light. "Feel better?"

She nodded, unable to speak.

"It really shook me when I saw you throw that guy. I felt like I'd failed you, like I should have been there to protect you. I hate that he hurt you. It won't ever happen again, Hayley. No one will ever hurt you again, I promise."

Hayley was shaken by the depth of emotion in his eyes. "Jace...I—"

"Shh, don't say anything for now. Just feel, sweetheart."

He took her in his arms, his mouth finding hers. Without thought or hesitation, Hayley opened her mouth to him as passion exploded between them. Jace's tongue swept inside her mouth and she welcomed it with bold, insistent caresses that pulled a rumbling groan from his throat.

Her arms wound around his shoulders and his tightened at her back. His hands swept slowly up and down, pulling her closer until her breasts were flattened against his chest. Jace sat back, his mouth never breaking contact as he pulled Hayley with him. She ended up half draped across his lap, her legs bent and laid out across the passenger side of the seat.

They continued to explore the warm, moist caverns of each other's mouths. Jace took one arm from behind her and moved to the front of her blouse, pulling the tattered piece free from where it was tucked under her bra strap. Retaining enough sanity to realize where he was headed, Hayley came up for air, her questioning gaze finding his.

The look in his eyes was incredible—fire, passion, need, all tightly leashed by a will of iron. His hand shook slightly as he traced the red strap of her bra downward. "I can't tell you how intrigued I am by this wispy little thing you're wearing. Are your panties all red and lacy too?"

Hayley flushed. "I like pretty things…and yes, they are."

"Oh, darlin', I like pretty things too. I especially like what's *in* them." His hand continued its journey until he cupped her breast in his hand. Hayley moaned and pushed into his touch. "That's it, darlin', just let it feel good."

Jace bent to her, his mouth fastening on the rigid nub of her nipple where it pressed against the lace. With his tongue flicking over the soft lace, he began to suckle. Hayley's body stiffened as she pushed into him, freely offering more. Her panting breaths and desperate whimpers rang through the air and her hips began to move in a needy, sensual rhythm that drew his hand down her torso and between her slightly open thighs.

Lost in the sensual fire and seeking the orgasm that was rapidly building inside her, Hayley spread herself for him. An animalistic moan reverberated from her as Jace's hand began a firm, rubbing stroke that caused a wave of heat to build and build. She arched against him, gasping when he released her nipple with a stinging nip. Once more his mouth settled against her throat, lips and tongue bestowing caresses that made her shiver. Jace moved higher. In a move that made her stomach clench and ripple with need, he licked the sensitive hollow beneath her ear before applying a gentle suction.

Her spine bowed. "Mmm, Jace, *please*."

"That's it, sugar. So good, so wild for me." The husky rasp of his voice sent sensation dancing across her nerve endings. "One day soon, I'm gonna have you in my bed. I'm gonna part these luscious thighs and sink my cock in so deep. Right here," Jace emphasized his words by increasing the pressure between Hayley's thighs. "Right here, darlin'. Gonna fuck you until you *scream*."

Hayley felt herself go up in a blaze of excruciating pleasure. With a wail she came, her hips undulating in a series of fast and slow movements that drew every ounce of pleasure from Jace's sure touch. All the tension that had built up during the evening drained from her body as she lay against him, slowly floating down from the pinnacle he'd taken her to. She drew deep shuddering breaths that finally slowed to normal. As they did, reality restored itself with a bang and she stiffened in his arms.

"It's all right," he murmured. "You were beautiful, Hayley, just beautiful."

She relaxed slightly but couldn't stop the wave of confusion and conflicting emotion that swept through her. "Jace, I'm sorry. I shouldn't have done that. I know you'll want me to...reciprocate, but I—"

Jace silenced her with a soft kiss. "I may *want*, but I don't *expect*. You're not ready and—much as I hate to admit it—I'm not ready either. At least not for anything beyond the physical. I'm more than ready for that." He chuckled. "I'm so ready it hurts, but there's more than just that between us and you and I need time." He helped her to sit up straight and adjust her clothes. "There are some things about me you need to know, things that are...complicated. So for right now, I'm going to walk you to your door and say good night. Okay?"

Hayley nodded her agreement, touched by Jace's sensitivity. She waited for him as he exited the truck, her slightly wide-eyed gaze following him as he walked around to open her door. When she stepped out, his arm slipped around her waist and she welcomed the warmth and security that flooded through her. They walked to the porch and Jace waited patiently while she dug her house key out of her pocket.

Upon opening the door, dim light spilled out from the lamp that rested on the hall table. It illuminated a section of the porch floor and sent its soft glow over them. Jace's expression was solemn.

He reached out and stroked her cheek. "Are you an open-minded woman, Hayley?"

"I like to think so," she replied softly, puzzled by the question.

"That's good to know," Jace acknowledged and leaned in to kiss her. It was a soft, sweet kiss filled with muted fire and promise. "Good night, sweetheart."

"Good night," she murmured and watched him walk to his truck.

She couldn't help the smile that pulled at her lips as she heard him mutter and surreptitiously adjust himself. As he jumped in his truck, she waved and closed the door, locking it firmly behind her.

Later that evening, Hayley was awakened by various muscles in her body cramping. She groaned and rolled over, pulling herself out of bed. She stood, swaying slightly, her sleep-fogged mind telling her that she must have strained her muscles when she'd flipped that rowdy bastard at Morgan's. With a muttered curse and groggy, shuffling steps, she entered the bathroom, filled a glass of water and downed a couple of maximum strength pain relievers.

Still half asleep, she stumbled back to bed, slid under the covers and immediately dozed off. In her half wakened state, she never thought to question the fact that she was able to see with perfect clarity in her pitch-dark bedroom.

* * * * *

The next day Hayley felt oddly ill at ease, as though she couldn't get comfortable in her own skin. Off and on, disturbing sensations seemed to ripple through her body, making her restless and uneasy. Strange yet compelling dreams had ruled her sleeping mind. One particularly vivid one rose above the rest and she contemplated it while sipping a cup a coffee at the kitchen table. Jace had called earlier to tell her about a client meeting he had to attend. She had nothing to distract her attention from the memory.

It was dark and she was outside walking in the woods. When she looked up through an open space in the canopy of tree limbs above, the sky was clear and the moon was shining. The opalescent light in combination with a soft breeze sent bizarre, threatening shadows dancing among the underbrush. It should have been frightening, but Hayley felt a strange blend of peace and contentment. A part of her knew with unshakable certainty that there was nothing in those shadows that could harm her. She belonged there among them, could even become a shadow herself if she so pleased.

Frowning, Hayley put her coffee cup down and closed her eyes. There was more to the dream than she had first thought and ever so slowly it was coming back.

She remembered walking, searching for something or someone. She wasn't afraid of being alone, but it felt wrong. There were others waiting and she belonged with them.

"Others?" Hayley whispered and shivered. Something about this dream made it seem almost real. Keeping her eyes closed, she took a deep breath and relaxed, opening herself to the images in her mind as they unfolded before her.

She increased her pace, constantly searching for something to show her the way. She found it. A scent that tickled her nostrils. It was strange yet oddly familiar. It beckoned to her, drawing her on until she broke through a thick stand of brush into a large clearing. Gathered there, eerily silent and still, was a pack of wolves. There was an air of anticipation swirling among them and Hayley knew she'd been expected. These were the others. This was where she belonged.

Hayley became aware of the fact that she was panting lightly. She fought to push the distraction away, to stay with the dream.

The wolves were beautiful, sleek and lithe under coats that ranged from hues of gray, charcoal, russet and ivory. They looked at her with eyes of pale yellow, dark golden brown and rust. For some reason she was unsurprised to see hues of green and blue as well, though something told her this wasn't natural for wolves.

At the far side of the clearing the wolves stirred. Slowly the pack drew apart to leave a pathway between Hayley and the wolf who had entered the clearing opposite her. Recognition rippled through her. She'd seen this wolf before. It was the black wolf who'd appeared at the pond the first night she arrived in Whispering Springs. His blue-green eyes held her regard. Her own eyes widened as his took on a soft ambient glow. Mesmerized, Hayley walked toward him through the parted wolf pack.

It was only when she was less than a few feet away that she realized something strange. She wasn't looking down at him or any of the other wolves. Her eyes were at the same level as theirs. She stopped and looked down. Where she'd expected to see her feet, instead were paws. Large, fur-covered paws with long, talon-like black nails. Heart pounding, Hayley swung her head back up. Blue-green eyes locked on hers. The wolf's head started to blur and the features of a man transposed themselves over that fur-covered muzzle.

"Jace."

At her soft whisper, Hayley snapped out of her daze. She sat stiffly in her chair, blinking her eyes, staring at the table. Taking a deep, shuddery breath, she forced her gaze out toward the sunshine streaming in through the kitchen window. Slowly she started to relax.

"Jeez, I know I have a vivid imagination, but come on. Jace may be a wolf, but he's an entirely human one," she murmured.

Rising from the chair, she took her cup to the sink and dumped the cold coffee down the drain. Hayley left the kitchen and got ready to go out.

Satisfied that her subconscious was simply spinning tales, she left the house, got in her car and headed toward the bookstore and Bryn.

For some reason she found herself anxious for company. Being alone just felt...wrong.

Chapter Five

The next few days passed uneventfully. Jace continued to work on the roof as he and Hayley fell into an easy camaraderie that included a lot of mutual teasing and an obvious growing affection. There was no repeat of that intense session that took place in Jace's truck. Jace made no secret of the fact that Hayley had his full and lustful attention, but it was tempered by a calm patience. His touches were light and his kisses were sweetly passionate in a way that caused her desire to kindle and burn.

From the hints he'd given her, Hayley knew he was working his way up to telling her something about himself. She couldn't deny the fact that she was intrigued, but she also found herself being unusually patient.

The two of them had clearly made the beginnings of a commitment to each other and were content, if only for this short time, to let their mutual desires build, to enjoy each other's company without any pressure and to allow things to move at their own pace. On the surface all appeared calm, yet underneath something primal was stirring in both of them. They both knew it was only a matter of time before it broke free, and both seemed determined to enjoy the building tension.

One afternoon, several days after the incident at Morgan's, Hayley was at the bookstore waiting to accompany Bryn to lunch. She sat in one of the customer relaxation nooks mulling over just how much she wanted to share with Bryn about what had happened between her and Jace and how things were progressing. On one hand she wanted to shout it to the rafters, but on the other, there was a tremulous joy in hugging the knowledge to herself.

It didn't occur to her that the constant smile she wore was a dead giveaway that something was up. Bryn and Clare had been nudging each other and exchanging smiles at Hayley's obvious distraction. Bryn had already spent the morning telling Clare about their adventure at Morgan's and about the obvious *something* that was developing between her sister and Jace.

The sound of the bell ringing over the door announced another customer and Hayley was pulled from her distracted reverie by the sound of Bryn's voice. Her normally welcoming tone carried a distinct chill.

"May I help you?"

"Well, now, that's real nice of you to ask. Too bad you weren't so accommodating the other night."

"Sir, may I remind you that this is a business establishment. If there's nothing you need in the way of reading material, I suggest you leave."

"Reading material, hmm? How about you fetch me a girlie magazine?"

"We don't sell that kind of literature here."

"Too high class for that, huh, little bitch?"

The man's insult brought Hayley and Clare charging to Bryn's defense. Each flanking her, they presented a united front against the three men who faced Bryn across the counter.

"Leave. Now," Clare ordered icily.

"And if we don't?" their leader challenged.

"I took care of you the other night. Don't make me repeat myself," Hayley threatened.

"There's no need for that," Clare told her, showing the cell phone in her hand. "I've already called 9-1-1."

The leader fixed his stare on Hayley. "I owe you, bitch, and I *always* pay my debts." Cursing them all with equal fervor, the man signaled his buddies and they left.

"What is it with that guy?" Hayley asked, shaken but determined to put on a brave face.

"His ego took a beating the other night and now he's out to prove something. He's trying to recover lost ground," Bryn answered.

"So that's the guy Hayley took out that night at Morgan's?" Clare asked, wide-eyed with concern.

"Yeah. Did you really call 9-1-1?" Hayley asked.

"No, but honestly? Maybe it wouldn't be a bad idea if we notified the sheriff. That guy and his pals could be dangerous."

Bryn frowned. "I don't want to stir up a bunch of trouble. And I especially don't want Logan to know about this." She held up a hand, stilling Clare's protest. "If something else happens, we'll call the sheriff's office and report it. Okay?"

Grudgingly, Clare agreed.

"Now, about lunch. Hayley, is it all right if we order something in and eat here? Not that I think they'll be back, but I don't want to leave Clare here alone."

"You know, you guys go ahead. I'm not feeling so great," Hayley confessed.

"What's wrong?"

"Strained muscles. I've been trying to ignore them, but this little episode has got me tensed up. I think I pulled something when I threw that guy the other night."

Her confession brought a chorus of commiserative ahhs, and they sent her on her way with various snippets of advice on how to get relief. Clare's declaration that a good soak in a hot tub filled with Jace would help brought a chorus of laughter. Hayley left with a smile on her slightly flushed face. As she drove home, she didn't notice the nondescript car that followed her at a discreet distance.

When she parked in her driveway beside Jace's truck, the car drove by at a slow pace. Attracted by the movement, she glanced over, absently noting the darkened windows, but dismissed it as soon as she turned toward the house. All she wanted at that moment was to curl up in bed around her heating pad.

She walked around to the back for a quick peek at the roof, but there was no sign of Jace, except for the ladder that still leaned against the house. Walking up the back steps, she opened the door and entered the kitchen to find Jace standing at the stove, stirring something in a pot.

"Hey, sweetheart, I thought you were having lunch with Bryn."

The day was overcast and cool, so Jace had remained fully dressed. His clothes bore the evidence of his hard work and a smudge of dirt marred his stubbled jaw. Even in her current, less than optimum state, Hayley was still very aware of the raw masculinity he projected. Irrational irritation manifested itself at the sight of him.

"Change of plans," she answered shortly.

"Well good, you can have lunch with me."

Biting her tongue and fighting to remain civil, Hayley began to walk past him. "I'm not hungry."

Jace reached out, hooked an arm through hers and pulled her close. "You're not mad that I'm using the kitchen, are you?"

Her sharp retort died a quick death. Jace's eyes were shadowed by an expression she'd never seen before—vulnerability. She instinctively knew that at this moment, his guard was down. She could easily hurt him, something she didn't want to do.

She took a deep, steadying breath. "I'm not angry with you. I don't mind at all that you're using the kitchen. You're welcome to anything here."

"Anything?" he asked with a twinkle in his eyes as his usual teasing expression returned.

"*Almost* anything," she answered then grimaced as a particularly nasty pain chose that moment to imitate a fist squeezing her insides.

"Are you okay, Hayley?"

"No, I've got to go lie down."

"What's wrong?" Jace asked with concern as he trailed her to her bedroom.

Hayley rummaged through the closet until she found her heating pad. She walked to the bedside and bent to plug the cord into the wall socket by the headboard. "I guess I pulled some muscles the other night, all right? I'll be fine. Jace, please, just go back to your lunch or work or whatever, okay?" Her final words were a plea.

Concern lit his eyes. "Is there anything I can do? Maybe you should see a doctor."

Hayley couldn't help the smile that tugged at her lips. She toed her shoes off. "I don't need a doctor. Would you mind bringing me a glass of water?"

"Sure," he said and rushed from the room, clearly not thinking of the closer water source in the bathroom.

Hayley took advantage of his absence to quickly pull off her jeans and shirt. She exchanged them for a pale, lavender sleep shirt with matching shorts. When Jace returned with the water, she was settling herself under a blanket.

"I could use that bottle of ibuprofen from medicine cabinet. Please?"

Jace brought the bottle and watched as she opened it and shook two into the palm of her hand. He handed her the glass of water and Hayley swallowed them down. "Thanks," she said with a sigh and settled down on her side, her back toward Jace. She adjusted the heating pad. "I wish I had two of these things," she muttered. "My back is killing me."

"Would it help if I rubbed it?"

Hayley turned her head and gave him a silent perusal. "Maybe, but no funny stuff, Jace, I really don't feel very well, okay?"

"No funny stuff," he promised and sat down on the bed.

Jace folded the blanket over, exposing the long line of Hayley's back. "Where does it hurt? Here?" He touched her mid-back.

"A little higher."

He let his fingers trail upward.

"There."

"All right, just relax. I'm going to push your shirt up."

Suiting actions to words, Jace pushed the back of Hayley's shirt up, exposing smooth, pale skin. Hayley shifted slightly, rolling a bit farther forward to give him better access. Placing his hands on her back, he began an easy massage and smiled at Hayley's groan of pleasure.

"Oh yeah, that feels goood."

"Glad you like it," he commented as he continued to work on her back.

He could feel the tension easing from Hayley's muscles as he worked. With one hand continuing its massage on the target area, he let his other hand wander farther up her back to her shoulders and the back of her neck. His touch was firm, his movements smooth, rhythmic, hypnotic. Enjoying the feel of Hayley's body under his hands, it took him a while to notice that she'd drifted off to sleep.

He continued to massage her lightly, gently easing his touch, then stopped. He pulled her shirt down and carefully tucked the blanket at her back. Jace sat quietly and let his gaze wander her profile as she slept. Her scent had changed. It was stronger, vibrantly ripe and compelling. He thought about it and realized that his strong reactions a few nights before had been due not only to the fact that Hayley was his mate but also that she was ovulating. If they'd had sex that night without some kind of protection, she'd be carrying his child.

The thought stirred something inside him, a welling of desire for something he'd never really thought about. Children. He'd never had much contact with them. His beta, Cade, led the young ones in the pack, teaching them etiquette, manners and what it meant to be part of the pack. Jace just looked on with amused tolerance.

He'd grown up with two sisters and, after his father died, spent years feeling responsible for their wellbeing. Perhaps that was why he'd never thought about fatherhood. When his mother remarried, the family responsibility went to someone else. He'd been free to behave as other young men did, wildly. For a long time he'd wanted no one depending on him.

In all his adventures with women he'd been very careful. Even though it would have been impossible for him to father a child with anyone other than his true mate, he took no unnecessary chances. He always used condoms, if only to send the message that the time he was spending with them was just fun and games. Nothing serious, no expectations.

Of course, he'd eventually grown up enough to realize that being responsible had its own rewards. He was a born leader. No one could lead properly without taking on a mantle of responsibility.

It struck him that he'd come full circle. He gone from the boy who'd been burdened with too much, to a young man who'd worked to unburden himself completely. Now he was a man, tough enough and strong enough that he sought out the responsibilities he'd once run from. His gaze refocused on Hayley and he pictured her pregnant, carrying their child. Unbidden, his cock began to rise. *Down, boy, now is not the time,* he thought to himself. He realized that the time *would* come and when it did, he was ready. He was ready for Hayley and everything that having her in his life would bring.

A warm wave of anticipation and satisfaction washed over him. He leaned over and kissed her gently on the temple. She stirred and mumbled.

"Shh, baby, sleep," he whispered, stood and quietly left the room.

* * * * *

Hayley stretched and yawned as she slowly awakened. She took in a deep breath and smiled. Jace was still here. She could smell his distinctive, masculine aroma as she took another deep breath and held it inside for a moment before letting it go. A slight frown marred her brow. How was it she could smell his scent so distinctly? She dismissed the question in spite of a niggling sliver of disquiet. It must have just lingered from when he was in her bedroom earlier.

She could hear the faint murmur of the television and smell a delicious aroma wafting into her room. Jace had obviously cooked something.

Her stomach rumbled as she rolled over and sat up. She turned off the heating pad and set it aside. Standing, she waited a second for any sign of muscle aches, but they were gone. A sigh of relief passed her lips and she walked into the bathroom to wash her hands, splash her face with water and run a brush through her hair.

Shrugging into a short robe, she wandered down the hall and entered the living room just as Jace emerged from the kitchen. He'd obviously gone home and cleaned up. Gone was the dirt-smudged face. He was freshly shaved and wore a clean pair of jeans, a white button-down shirt with the tails tucked in and white athletic shoes.

"I heard you get up. Dinner's ready. You hungry?" he asked with an inquiring smile.

"Starving. Did you actually cook?"

"Sort of."

"Sort of?"

"It's my shortcut casserole."

Hayley grinned. "What's that?"

"I buy a baked chicken from the deli, cut it up and lay it out in a pan, pour broccoli-cheese and rice soup over it, shove it in the oven along with some heat-and-serve dinner rolls and twenty minutes later, dinner is served," he explained proudly.

"Very clever," she chuckled. "It smells delicious."

"It is," he asserted confidently. "Right this way, sweetheart."

Jace ushered her into the kitchen and pulled a chair out for her. He'd already set the table with plates, silverware and glasses. In addition, there was a nice tablecloth and even a lit candle in a jar placed in the center.

"Wow, this is really nice, Jace," Hayley complimented as she took her seat.

With a flourish, Jace placed the serving dish with his casserole on the table and added a covered basket containing the rolls. "Didn't figure you'd feel like cooking, and since you missed lunch, I decided I'd better feed you before I go. You were lookin' a mite pale, sweetheart."

Hayley lowered her eyes suddenly feeling a bit bashful. "Thank you for earlier, you really made me feel better."

"You're welcome," he replied. "I could tell by the way you were snoring."

"I do not snore!"

Jace laughed. "Just teasing. Now here, try this."

She directed a quelling frown his way as he placed a healthy helping of casserole on her plate. Hayley picked up her fork, brought a small bite to her mouth and took a tentative taste.

She smiled. "You didn't lie—it *is* good."

"Of course."

Jace filled their glasses from a frosty pitcher of lemonade then seated himself. They passed the dinner rolls and butter. He'd also heated up some canned sweet corn, which Hayley confessed was her favorite vegetable. They enjoyed a relaxed meal and chatted easily. Hayley asked Jace about his work and he reciprocated.

The time passed pleasantly and more quickly than either thought possible. There was something homey and welcoming about the whole thing that both of them were enjoying immensely.

Jace looked at his watch. "I'm going to start cleaning up. I have to get going soon. I have a business meeting this evening."

"With Gracie Stevens?" Hayley blurted out, and then wished she'd bitten her tongue at the expression on Jace's face.

He stood and quietly gathered their empty plates and put them in the sink. Turning back, he gave her a steady look. "No, with the city planning council. We're drawing up plans to enlarge the library."

He turned the water on and let it fill the sink before he spoke again, his back to her. "I know what my reputation is, Hayley. I don't deny it. I earned it, I know that." He paused and frowned as though searching for the right words. "I've never cooked for anyone. I've never touched a woman just to soothe and ease her pain. Everything I've ever done, when it came to a woman, was with one goal in mind. Sex."

Jace turned back to face her. "Now don't get me wrong, where you're concerned I definitely want sex. Fast, slow, hot, wet, any and every way we can do it sex—but I want something more too. I want to *make love* with you. I've never wanted to make love with a woman before. I've never wanted other things as well."

"What things?" Hayley whispered, shaken by his intensity.

"Things it's too early to talk about," he answered softly. "But I want you to know that I'm serious here. I'm not just fucking around. Damn!" He turned back to the sink and began washing the dishes with agitated movements. "This is important and I can't find the right words. You're turning me inside out!"

Hayley sat in silence for a moment, her heart beating strongly, her breath rushing in her lungs and tears stinging her eyes. Jace's words brought on an emotional reaction of such strength she was near to being overwhelmed by it. She forced herself to calm and let her gaze slide the length of his body.

He was clearly tense, the muscles in his shoulders bunched with each move as he washed the dishes. Feeling the shock of Jace's declaration recede, Hayley let herself relax. With the relaxation came acceptance and affection and the need to put him at ease as well.

She rose from the chair and walked behind him. Reaching up, she placed her hands on his shoulders and felt him tense under her fingertips. "I'm sorry," she apologized softly and began to massage his hard muscles. "And you *did* find the right words—beautiful words, Jace."

Hayley let her hands slide down his back, over his rib cage and around his body, then brought her own body tight against his back as she hugged him fiercely. She felt his rumble of pleasure vibrate through both of them and with a smile lifted her cheek from where it rested against his back. Lifting up on tiptoes, she nuzzled the back of his neck and teased him with warm kisses.

A different kind of tension entered Jace's body. She smiled with satisfaction and sent her hands roaming over his chest. Her fingertips found and teased the tightening nubs of his nipples and Jace groaned, his breath beginning to pump in and out of his lungs at a greater speed.

Leaving one hand to tease a hard nipple, she let the other slide south over his rippled abs until it reached the top button of his jeans. Her fingers nimbly unhooked the first button, then the second and were reaching for the third when Jace's hand closed over hers.

He held on to her and turned in her arms. "What are you doing, Hayley?" he growled.

"Touching you," she purred.

"You don't have to do this."

"Well, I know *that*," she answered as though speaking to a simpleton. "If I *had* to, it wouldn't be nearly as much fun."

"If you're doing this because of what I said, I wish you wouldn't. It feels like you're rewarding me for being a good boy," he grumbled.

Hayley sighed. "You are such a contradiction, Jace McKenna. Now listen to me. Yes, I liked what you said. Yes, I appreciate your cooking for me. Yes, I appreciate how you rubbed my back and made me feel better. But it's more than that, I...I have *feelings* for you. You annoy me and you make my heart beat faster and sometimes I feel like I want to kick your ass or just kiss you cross-eyed. And right now, at this moment, all I can think about is how sweet you are and how sexy and how I just need to touch you. So let me touch you. Please?"

She noted the movement of Jace's throat as he swallowed and the glistening sheen that filled his eyes right before a warm, gentle glow ignited in their depths. "I'd say 'take me, I'm yours', but this is a serious moment, right?"

Hayley grinned and chuckled. "Very serious." She looked around as though considering the possibilities then pushed him back against the counter. "This'll do for starters," she murmured, and initiated a teasing, wet kiss, filled with languorous strokes of her tongue.

Jace groaned and opened for her, his tongue meeting hers, emulating its slow, sinuous movements. Hayley's hands moved over his shoulders and arms, caressing the hard muscles that bunched under his shirt. Continuing the kiss and moving her hands to his chest, she started at the top, unbuttoned his shirt and pulled it from under the waistband of his jeans. She spread the fabric wide to expose his chest and ran her fingers through the silky, dark hair she found there.

"I've wanted to do this since that first day I saw you with your shirt off. Do you have any idea how damn sexy this is?" she murmured against his lips as her fingertips raked over him.

"I didn't, but now I do," he answered softly and gasped as she lightly pinched the tiny nubs of his nipples. "Damn, babe," he moaned.

"Mmm, I like it that your nipples are so sensitive. When you touch mine it feels like bolts of electricity shoot straight to my pussy," she whispered. "Do you feel it here?" she asked, one hand moving down to cup the growing bulge between his legs.

"Oh yeah," he groaned and pushed against her hand.

"Good, I want to know everything that makes you feel good."

She began kissing him again while her hands busied themselves unbuttoning the final buttons on his jeans. She pushed them down his hips, exposing his bright white briefs. Breaking the kiss by trailing her lips down to his chin, she nipped him playfully and looked down at what was revealed.

Clearly visible behind his briefs, his fully erect cock begged for release. "Oh my, now I know why they call it a treasure trail," she commented reverently as her fingertips drifted down the silky path of hair leading to his eager cock. Jace's stomach muscles tensed under her light caress and his breathing began to grow labored.

Using both hands, Hayley pulled the waistband of his briefs out and down, revealing Jace's thick, swollen length. "Jackpot," she breathed and smiled at Jace's breathless, involuntary chuckle.

She slid her hands around his body and pushed his jeans and briefs down past the taut cheeks of his ass, making sure to get a lingering handful of each tempting mound. Bending down, she untied his shoes and pulled them off. "Jump up on the counter," she ordered.

Jace raised an eyebrow but obeyed without question. Hayley pulled his jeans and briefs completely off, draping them over a nearby kitchen chair.

"Mmm, perfect," Hayley murmured and moved between his thighs.

Jace leaned down for a kiss, which Haley was more than willing to give. Her mouth again found his and the kisses intensified — hot, tongue-sizzling affairs that blurred the mind and built desire to a fever pitch. When she broke the kiss, her mouth headed south, finding the treasure trail and following it to her reward. Jace's cock stood straight and tall, staring boldly at her approach, and Hayley smiled at its brazenly masculine display.

She wet her lips and met the large, mushroom-shaped head with a wet lingering kiss that slid over and around the entire area before opening her mouth and taking it inside. Jace groaned, jumped and leaned back, banging his head on the cupboard behind him.

Hayley pulled off and straightened. Reaching out, she cupped the back of his head. "Are you okay, baby?" she asked, lightly massaging his scalp.

"I'm good," he replied, his voice thick and husky.

"Is it okay if I go back to what I was doing?" she teased.

"Please," Jace answered, a note of desperation in his voice.

Hayley barely restrained her smile as she bent to him and again took his cock in her mouth. The feel of him was incredible. She hummed with pleasure as her tongue and mouth took in the flavors and textures of Jace. She could see the gnarled veins that wrapped his length and feel the throbbing of his heart in the blood that filled it. His skin was satiny-soft, a sharp contrast to the iron-hard column it covered.

She slowly stroked up and down the shaft then released him and ran her tongue down the underside to his scrotum.

His body exuded heat and with it, his scent. Hayley buried her face between his thighs and breathed deeply of his testosterone-laden musk. The heady aroma caused her head to whirl and her pussy to clench, forcing a deep moan from the depths of her chest. Her hands aggressively pushing his thighs farther apart as her tongue bathed his heavily laden balls before taking one into her mouth, where she rolled it around, sucking and licking before releasing it. Taking the other one inside her mouth, she repeated the procedure. Jace was moaning, his thighs tensing as his hips instinctively lifted to her clever mouth.

Again she slid her tongue up the long length of his cock and looked up, meeting his hot, hungry gaze. His face wore an expression of desperation as though trying to keep the pleasure at bay. Hayley took him back inside and he groaned, his lips parting while sharp pants and small expressions of pleasure uncontrollably issued from them. His hips undulated and she went with the rhythm, allowing him to slide his cock back and forth in her mouth at whatever speed pleased him. Sliding her mouth up and off, she replaced it with her hand and kept a steady, even stroke as she again took his lips in a sizzling kiss. Their tongues met and mated, twining together in a wet, sensual dance.

A deep guttural groan vibrated between them and Hayley swallowed the sound before releasing his lips. "Hayley, babe, I'm going to come," he bit out harshly.

Eagerly, Hayley bent and engulfed his red, throbbing tip, her mouth stroking, her tongue caressing the highly sensitized underside of his cock. She felt his cock swell even more before the first volley of his hot, creamy semen hit her tongue. She swallowed his salty-sweet essence again and again as successive spurts filled her mouth. Above her Jace was shuddering and groaning out his pleasure, his hands in her hair, holding her, his fingers tightening and loosening convulsively.

Hayley held him gently in her mouth. Knowing how sensitive he would be after coming, she applied gossamer-light strokes with her tongue to finish him off then slowly released him. Jace let his hands fall away and Hayley rose up to stare at his face. His eyes were closed, his intense expression slowly relaxing to normal. With his eyes still closed, he reached out and pulled her close, his mouth seeking hers.

Hayley moaned with pleasure as his tongue slowly explored her mouth, seeking and tasting. It pleased her that he wasn't afraid to taste himself and she snuggled into him, gladly giving all he wanted.

Jace pulled away and heaved a sated sigh, his eyes opening and meeting hers. Hayley watched his eyes widen with shock that he quickly squelched. "Is something wrong?" she asked.

Jace hugged her fiercely. "Not at all, in fact, everything's pretty damn good. How about you, are you feeling okay?"

She nodded, returned his hug and noted the time on the clock above her refrigerator. "What time's your meeting?"

"Eight."

"You have ten minutes to get there."

"Shit!"

Jace eased her aside and jumped off the counter, feverishly dressing and replacing his shoes. Hayley watched him with an amused smile tugging at her lips.

"Think this is funny, huh?" he questioned, giving her a narrow-eyed look as he sat tying the final shoelace.

"Yeah," she confessed with a chuckle.

He rose and took her in his arms, kissing her soundly. "Payback's gonna be hell, sweetheart." He gave her a swat on the backside and headed for the door. He paused before going out and turned back to look at her. "Hayley...I... Damn! Tomorrow we're having a serious talk, all right?"

She nodded, and noting the odd mix of excitement and worry in his eyes, a small shiver of anxiety crept up her spine, but she managed to hide it and smile. "You know where to find me."

Jace strode back in, giving her a quick and fiercely possessive kiss before bolting for the door. Hayley locked it behind him and bit her lip—something was definitely on that man's mind, and she knew she was going to be uneasy until all was revealed.

Chapter Six

ജ

Jace sat behind the wheel of his truck staring at the house for a moment before starting the engine and heading for his meeting. He was glad Logan was going to be there. This totally unexpected turn of events had shaken him, and he was riding a wave of elation that also threatened to send him crashing if Hayley didn't accept what he had to tell her.

His stomach clenched at the thought. "Please God, don't let her reject it. Damn, how the hell did this happen?" he murmured.

He arrived at city hall and made his way to the city planner's office, noting that he was the last to arrive. He was greeted by the others already there and took a seat next to Logan.

"You're late," Logan commented softly as the meeting began.

"Something unexpected came up."

"Since you're not walking funny, I assume it also went down?"

"You missed your true calling. You should have been a comedian," Jace commented sourly.

Logan grinned. "That's what Bryn tells me. I'll have to look into that."

Jace rolled his eyes. "Seriously though, I've got a problem I need to talk with you about. It involves Hayley."

Logan was instantly serious. "After the meeting?"

"Yeah."

There was no more time for chitchat as Jace was called on to go over the blueprints and explain in detail the renovations planned for the library. The meeting went quickly as they were in the final stages of approving the plans. Everyone was pleased to come to an early and unanimous agreement.

As the meeting came to a close, Clare's husband, Brian Harrelson, approached Logan and Jace and without preliminaries told them, "We've got a problem."

"What is it?" Logan asked, assuming it pertained to the meeting.

"Yesterday, that guy Bryn and Hayley had trouble with at Morgan's showed up at the bookstore with a couple of friends. He started harassing the girls. He threatened Hayley, told her he owed her and he always paid his debts."

"Son of a bitch. Bryn didn't say a word," Logan fumed.

Jace was speechless, his anger and alarm running so deep he couldn't speak.

"Clare didn't want to tell me, but I could see she was worried about something when she got home yesterday. I finally got it out of her," Brian told them. "I know you don't like this any more than I do. I think we should notify the sheriff to keep an eye out for these guys."

Jace found his tongue. "Agreed. Brian, will you take care of that part of it? In the meantime, I'm going to call in some favors and see if we can locate where these guys are staying. I think it's time to show them how unwelcome their presence is in Whispering Springs."

"Just one thing," Brian added before leaving. "If you find these guys? I want to be there."

"You got it," Jace agreed and slapped him on the back. He turned to find Logan giving him a gimlet-eyed stare. "What? Don't tell me you don't want a piece of these guys."

They'd made their way out to the parking lot and Logan's eyes took on a sparkling glow that was clearly seen in the darkness. "You know my first reaction is to rip this guy's head off." He took a deep breath and the fire in his eyes banked to a wavering ember. "But that's why I'm pack liaison. I don't go with my first reaction, unlike some hotheaded alphas I know."

Jace grimaced and ran an agitated hand through his hair. "Damn it, Logan, you know I'm trying to rein myself in. When was the last time I started something you had to fix?"

"It's been a while, and don't think I don't appreciate it— but we have to keep our heads here. Much as I'd like to inflict some damage, you know what kind of trouble that could bring." Logan held up his hand to forestall Jace's protest. "But that doesn't mean we can't scare the crap out of them," he suggested with an evil chuckle.

Jace grinned, noting the glow in Logan's eyes, fueled by his excitement. It reminded him of his current dilemma. "About that problem that concerns Hayley?"

"Go on."

"She's becoming one of us."

Logan hooted and slapped Jace on the back. "Congratulations! Have you told Bryn?"

"That's just the problem," he answered, giving Logan an uncomfortable look. "I haven't told Hayley."

"*What?* What the hell does that mean? How could you not tell her? You just turned her without saying a word?"

"No! It's not like that. I don't know how it happened. We were, um, fooling around earlier and when we finished, Hayley's eyes were glowing. It shocked the hell out of me."

"Just what kind of fooling around are we talking about here? Intercourse?"

"No, that's just it, Logan. We haven't mated yet," Jace confessed, a bit red-faced at Logan's look of surprise. "I've been giving her time to get to know me," he explained, leaving out the part about working his courage up to tell her about his being a werewolf. "There's been kissing and touching and some oral stuff most recently, but no biting, no mating, nothing more."

"Jace, this doesn't make sense. At some point while Hayley was ovulating, your saliva had to come into contact with her bloodstream."

Jace suddenly felt as though he'd been hit by a bolt of lightning. "Oh my God," he whispered as understanding dawned in his eyes. "That night at Morgan's, when she got that scratch on her throat. When I took her home, I noticed it had started bleeding again. I licked the wound clean. Today, I could tell she was ovulating. I remember thinking that was why my reactions were so strong that night." He looked at Logan with a growing horror. "I didn't think about it. I just reacted to the wound. I wanted to make it feel better. I changed her without her permission! Without even telling her who and *what* I really am, without telling her she's my mate. Christ, Logan! What have I done? If she doesn't accept this she's going to hate me."

Logan stood silently for a moment considering his answer then placed a hand on Jace's shoulder and gave it a squeeze before releasing him. "Do you love Hayley?"

"Of course I do. How can you even ask? She's everything to me now."

"How do you think she feels about you?"

Jace thought a moment before answering. "I'm pretty sure she's feeling some of the same."

Logan nodded. "Then let's not jump the gun. You love her, she's beginning to love you. Give it a chance to work itself out, but the first thing you need to do is *tell her*."

"I know, I've been working up to it, but you know from personal experience how difficult it is. If she rejects my other nature, I'm fucked. No lover, no wife, no children. I could live without the children, but I don't want to live without Hayley," he confessed. "There's never been a time in my life when I wished I wasn't a werewolf, but I could almost wish for it now."

"Well, that's not going to happen, so do what you do best. Fight for her. Show her all the magic this state of being brings. If that doesn't persuade her, then the fact that she loves you should."

"I hope to hell you're right."

"It'll work out, Jace."

"That's what I'm worried about. That it'll work out *wrong*."

Logan shook his head. "I know. Listen, I've got to get home. I have a mate to rake over the coals for keeping secrets from me."

Jace managed a halfhearted smile. "Her co-conspirator has earned some chastisement too."

Logan chuckled and slapped him on the back. "Good night, Jace. If there's anything I can do, well, you know how to reach me."

"Thanks, Logan. Good night."

The two friends parted company, climbed into their respective vehicles and drove away. As he drove back to Hayley's, Jace replayed the events of the evening, his mind whirling with confusion, anxiety and anger. He'd been dreading the thought of finally telling Hayley about his true nature and having to deal with her reaction. Feeling this unsure of himself had greatly unsettled him. Jace was no coward. He'd faced every difficult situation head on, but for this one. He felt a growing anger with himself.

Now he not only had to deal with the consequences of his indecision—after having accidentally turned Hayley, he had to deal with a truckload of guilt. To top it all off, she was keeping secrets from him. Secrets that could endanger her life. He grudgingly acknowledged the fact that they were not at the stage where Hayley would know that she was to rely on him for protection. Yet he unreasonably felt as though she distrusted his ability to do so. Her failure to come to him left him feeling as though she had judged him inadequate to handle the situation.

That line of thought knotted his tangled emotions and fueled his anger to the point that by the time he reached Hayley's house, he wasn't sure which way was up. He was mad as hell and spoiling for a fight. Exiting his truck, he strode up the porch steps and, upon reaching the door, pounded loudly on that shivering panel.

Having heard his truck pull up, Hayley was already at the door. "Hey, take it easy on the door, buddy," she teased as she opened it to let him in.

Unsmiling, Jace stalked in and very deliberately closed the door. "Did you really think I wouldn't find out?" he questioned harshly, his eyes glowing like heated lava.

Hayley frowned. "Find out what?"

"You had some *visitors* at the bookstore this morning."

"Oh that. It's no big deal."

"No big deal. No big *deal*? That man intends to harm you and you think it's no big deal?" Jace gave her a disbelieving stare. "Why don't you tell me the real reason you didn't want me to know, Hayley."

"All right, fine," she bit out, her own eyes beginning to blaze. "Bryn and I knew that you and Logan would overreact, just like you're doing right now. I suppose Logan is giving Bryn the third degree right this very moment."

"You got that right. Logan won't stand for his mate keeping secrets from him and neither will I."

Hayley frowned. "What do you mean by *mate*?"

Jace's anger was momentarily arrested but he quickly recovered. "It's just a word, Hayley, another term for wife or lover. Don't try to distract me. You and I both know you weren't afraid I'd overreact to the news. The real reason you didn't tell me about that man threatening you is because you don't trust me. You don't think I'm man enough to handle it for you."

"*What?* That's bullshit and you know it, Jace McKenna. I don't *believe* this. You rush over here all angry and indignant trying to make me feel like I've done something wrong, when all you want is your ego stroked. I thought you were a man, not a little boy."

A flood of fury swept all good sense from Jace's head. He grabbed her arm, pulling her close. "The only thing I wanted *stroked* got taken care of earlier, babe. Your senses must be impaired if you couldn't tell it was a *man* you sucked off."

Hayley's face blanched, her breath coming in shaky pants. "Get out," she ordered.

"Gladly," Jace replied bitterly. Releasing her arm, he spun on his heel and opened the door, slamming it behind him. Reaching his truck, he jumped in, started the engine and revved it before popping it in gear and peeling out of her driveway. He headed straight for Morgan's.

* * * * *

"Two-fucking-forty-three in the morning," Cade D'jorlin growled as he looked at the clock by his bed. "If one of those cubs is in trouble again, I swear I'm gonna peel his hide." He picked up the ringing telephone. "D'jorlin."

"Cade, it's David Morgan."

"Son of a *bitch*. Which one is it this time, Dave?"

Dave chuckled. "Well actually, it's our alpha."

"Jace?"

"That's the one."

"I'll be right there."

Cade rolled out of bed and walked with just the barest hint of a limp to the bathroom. Comfortable in the dark, he used the toilet, washed his hands and splashed water on his face before picking up the bottle of mouthwash by the sink and taking a swig. He swished it around before spitting it back in the sink then ran the water to rinse it down. Picking up his

hairbrush, he gave his short blond hair a couple of swipes—
not that there was much to be brushed. Cade kept his hair
short, a habit ingrained from his time as a Marine.

Heading back to the bedroom, he reached down for the
pair of jeans he'd thrown on the floor by the bed. Knowing
they were clean, he pulled them on, sans underwear, liking the
feel of the denim against his skin. He stood, went to the closet
and pulled out a hunter green t-shirt, slipping it over his head
and skimming it down his muscled torso.

Grabbing his keys off the dresser, he walked through the
house, stopping to slip on his shoes, then let himself into the
garage. Only then did he flip on a light and paused to admire
the shine on his baby. The black 1982 model Corvette in cherry
condition awaited him, and Cade lost no time in seating
himself behind the wheel. He sighed with pleasure. The seat fit
like a glove.

"At least I get *some* pleasure in being pulled out of bed in
the middle of the night," he muttered as he headed down the
road to Morgan's.

Cade made the trip in fifteen minutes and pulled into the
lot, noting that Jace's truck and David's car were the only two
vehicles present. He parked by Jace's truck and got out,
locking his door behind him. More than familiar with
Morgan's, he entered and—seeing no one around—headed to
the back office. David was there alone, going over some
invoices.

"Hey, Dave, where is he?"

"Upstairs. Glad you're here, Cade." Dave rose and led the
way back out front. "I wasn't so much worried about him
driving—you know how fast the effects of alcohol wear off on
us, and I could keep him here until they do—but something's
bothering him. He's not saying what, but I think he needs to
talk, and who better than you or Logan?"

Cade followed Dave and they halted at the foot of the stairs. Cade slapped Dave on the back. "I'll take it from here. Thanks."

"No problem. I'm headed home. Lock up when you leave. Okay?"

"You got it."

Cade climbed the stairs. It was the first time he'd ever done so without the jukebox wailing, and he smiled at the heretofore unnoticed creaks. His ears also picked up the sound of quiet singing. At least it was *supposed* to be singing.

Little Jace, one-note, he thought with an irreverent grin.

Reaching the top floor, he spotted Jace sprawled out in the furthermost booth. The table was littered with shredded and wadded-up napkins scattered amongst empty bottles. It looked as though he'd started with beer, then graduated to whiskey shots straight from the bottle—several bottles in fact.

A bleary-eyed Jace spotted Cade. "Hey, Cade, ol' buddy. Sit down, brother wolf, and have a drink. Have a bunch of drinks. I did." He let out a belch and a drunken chuckle.

Cade walked up to the booth and moved some of the empties over before taking the seat opposite Jace. "Hey, boss, how you doin'?"

"Shitty, and that's the God's honest truth."

Cade's brows rose. He was surprised Jace confessed to having a problem so easily. He'd been sure it would take a while to weasel it out of him. "So what's the trouble? It's not like you to resort to this," he observed, his glance taking in all the empties.

"I fucked up, Cade, I fucked up bad. I hurt Hayley and now she hates me. My mate hates me." Arms on the table, Jace hung his head, his shoulders slumping.

"Why don't you tell me what happened?"

Jace started, his explanation at first a confused ramble, but by the time he was finished, he was dead sober.

"Well, how 'bout that. You really *are* in love. When it comes to women you're usually the original Mr. Smooth." Cade smiled. "But you really put your foot in your mouth this time. Hell, you swallowed it whole."

Jace groaned. "You're not helping."

Cade chuckled. "I'll tell you what. Think about this. Here you are, feeling guilty as hell and messing yourself up because you hurt Hayley's feelings. Right?"

Jace nodded.

"Seems to me she said some harsh words to you too, especially that 'I thought you were a man' remark. What do you wanna bet she's feeling some guilt of her own?"

"You think?" Jace asked hopefully.

"Oh yeah. You see, the thing with women is, unlike men who run out and get drunk, they start thinking about what happened. They pick it apart and analyze every word and every gesture to try to figure out just what went wrong. They obsess about it until they're sure they've wrung every little bit of information they can out of it. And in this case, unless she's a cast-iron bitch with no heart who's determined to make everything your fault, I'd bet money on the fact that she's feeling just as bad as you are."

Jace considered Cade's words for a moment then actually found a small smile tugging at his lips. "How'd you learn so much about women?"

"I was actually in love once. Trouble is, she turned out to be a cast-iron bitch."

"You never told me that."

"Some things are better left forgotten. You ready to go home?"

"Yeah."

They both slid out of the booth and headed downstairs. Cade pulled the door shut, making sure it locked behind them. The sun was just beginning to rise as they walked to their vehicles. A cool, fresh breeze brought the morning's aromas to their heightened senses. Jace took a deep breath, pushing the last of the fuzz from his head.

"Thanks, Cade. Sorry I got you out of bed so early."

"No problem, boss. By the way, next time you try to sing, let me know and I'll bring you a bucket. Although I doubt it would help."

Jace growled. "Very funny. You and Logan should team up. You'd make a great comedy duo."

Cade laughed. "I'll have to discuss that with him."

He unlocked his car door, opened it and slid inside. With a wave, he took off down the road. Jace sat in his truck for a moment, thinking about Cade's words and making a few plans. With a hopeful attitude, he started his truck and headed for home.

* * * * *

Hayley had been doing exactly what Cade had predicted. She was going over the fight with a fine-toothed comb. After Jace left, she'd fumed and roundly cursed every hair on his head. Every time she thought about the crass remark he'd made, a twinge of pain twisted something inside her. Like a sore tooth, she couldn't leave the incident alone. Her mind spun through the whole thing from start to finish, again and again, until she felt dizzy with it.

Finally she fixed herself a cup of tea, forced herself to sit down on the sofa and began some deep breathing exercises she'd learned to alleviate stress. With her thoughts finally calm and focused, she began to really think about what had happened. Not only that, she began to think about Jace, about who he was and what she knew about him.

It began to dawn on her that Jace would never deliberately hurt her. The remark he'd made was a result of her own runaway tongue. Instead of focusing on what the real problem had been, she'd fired the first volley of insults that caused their disagreement to degenerate to the point it had.

"Damn," she murmured and cringed at the thought of what she'd said.

Jace had been upset because she'd been threatened and because she hadn't told him about it. In hindsight she supposed it *could* be misconstrued that she didn't trust him to help her handle it, but the idea of Jace thinking that she would believe he wasn't man enough was totally ludicrous. The man wasn't using his head and she began to wonder just why that was.

Deciding she needed to talk to someone, she picked up the phone and hit the speed dial for Bryn. "Hey," she spoke when Bryn picked up on the other end. "Are you busy? Jace and I had a fight. I need to talk." She listened for a moment. "Okay, I'll be there in a few minutes."

Twenty minutes later she sat in Bryn and Logan's kitchen with a cup of coffee, relating the sordid details of the fight. Afterward she looked at them expectantly.

"Well," Bryn told her. "You two really did a number on each other."

"I know that. And you don't have to tell me that I started the argument on its downhill slide. I never should have said what I said. I realize now that Jace was worried about me. That's why he was so angry. What I don't get is how he could ever think that I would think he's not man enough to handle anything."

"When a man's in love, he doesn't always behave rationally. The thinking processes sometimes go askew," Logan interjected.

Hayley and Bryn turned their wide-eyed gazes to him. "In love?" Hayley questioned. "What makes you think he's in love?"

"Aside from the fact that he told me, which by the way you did *not* hear from me, I think it's fairly obvious. Jace is a smart, levelheaded guy who's always been confident and in charge in any situation. Most especially where women are concerned. You come along and all of a sudden, he's acting like an idiot." Hayley smiled and Bryn snickered. "Only love does that to a man."

"He really said he loves me?"

Logan captured Hayley's gaze, his own filled with concern. "You really need to hear this from Jace. I'm only telling you because I think the two of you need a little help right now. It bothers me to see the two of you hurting each other." Hayley's eyes filled with tears. "I'm hoping this is an incident you'll both learn something from. When there's a problem, you need to talk it out rationally, not insult each other."

Hayley nodded, thoroughly chastised, as Bryn looked at Logan, pride and love clearly showing in her eyes. "You never cease to amaze me," she told him softly. "You're going to make such a wonderful father."

Logan's smile was almost bashful. "I'm really looking forward to it."

"Before this descends into a mush fest," Hayley commented with a smile, "I have one more question." Capturing their attention, she continued. "Jace made a strange remark during our argument. He said, and I quote, 'Logan won't stand for his *mate* keeping secrets from him, and neither will I'." She noted the look Bryn and Logan gave each other. "What did he mean by that?"

"That I shouldn't have kept what happened from Logan," Bryn said. "Which I know was wrong," she added in deference to his pointed look.

"That's not the part I mean. I'm talking about that word— *mate*."

"It's a common term. Some people refer to their spouse as their mate."

"I know that, but it seemed as though he meant something else, something more. Especially in light of the fact that he and I aren't married."

Logan rose from his chair, taking his cup to the sink and rinsing it out. "That's something you're going to have to discuss with Jace. I think Bryn and I have interfered enough. Don't you, babe?"

"Yes, I do," she agreed and took her own cup to the sink, rinsed it out then stood by Logan's side. She slipped an arm around his waist and the two of them presented a united front to Hayley, who took the hint.

"All right, I'll talk to Jace. After we set things right." She pushed her coffee cup over to Bryn who rinsed it and set it with the others. She rose and gave Bryn and Logan each a hug. "Thanks for listening and not letting me get away with anything."

"Always happy to show you the error of your wicked ways," Bryn teased.

"What a perfect sister," Hayley mocked and walked out of the kitchen to the front door. Logan and Bryn followed, said their goodbyes and saw her on her way.

"Do you think those two will ever get it together?" Bryn asked, leaning back into Logan.

He wrapped his arms around her. "I think they've both learned a valuable lesson. Communication, not castigation, is the key. And speaking of getting it together..." He bent and nuzzled her neck, biting that place between her neck and shoulder that always sent shivers down her spine. "How about we do just that?"

She pushed her bottom back against him, rubbing sensuously against the growing bulge in his jeans. "Umm, I'm in."

Logan spun her around and picked her up. Cradling her in his arms, he climbed the stairs to their bedroom. "Actually,

I'll be the one who's in," he murmured against her ear before nipping the lobe.

Bryn moaned. "Sounds good to me, just hurry."

Logan picked up the pace, reached the top of the stairs and strode into the bedroom. Soon the only sounds heard were soft whispers, moans and the rhythmic creaking of the bed.

Chapter Seven

❧

At nine-thirty that morning, there was a knock at Hayley's front door. She rose from her desk, her stomach clenching, thinking it might be Jace. When she opened the door, it was to find a delivery person holding a very large mixed bouquet of flowers in a crystal vase. She accepted the flowers and, taking them inside, she placed them on her desk. There was a small card. She took it from the envelope and read *Forgive me? Jace.*

The bouquet was a beautiful mix of pastel flowers, pink roses, white statis, yellow chrysanthemums, white daisies with yellow centers, pale pink delphiniums and some small lavender flowers she was unfamiliar with. She smiled as she looked at it and got a bit misty-eyed. Jace *was* going to apologize and she was going to get the chance to do so too. Sitting there, she was struck by the need to do something too. Picking up the phone, she put her own order in at the florist.

Two hours later the phone rang. Hayley picked it up and said hello.

"Did you get my flowers?"

"Yes, I did. Did you get my plant?"

"Yes, I did. Does this mean I'm forgiven?"

"Yes. Do you forgive me?"

"There's nothing to forgive, sweetheart. I was totally out of line."

"Jace, I started it. I should have never said what I said to you."

"I shouldn't have come charging over there all pissed off…but I was worried about you."

"I know you were and it makes me feel good to know you care. I should have told you what happened."

There was a significant pause and they both laughed. "I guess we finally agree on something," Hayley commented.

"See, I knew it could happen if we just worked on it a little bit."

"I guess you were right."

"Hayley, sweetheart, I want to see you so bad. If I could, I'd be there now instead of calling. Truth is, I'm on a job and things are at a critical stage right now."

"It's okay. The most important thing is knowing everything's all right between us."

"I know what you mean. I feel a lot better now. Hold on a sec." Hayley could hear a conversation taking place between Jace and another man. "Sweetheart, I've got to go, these people are driving me nuts. I'll talk to you soon, all right?"

"All right. Bye."

Hayley hung up the phone and sighed. She'd told the truth when she'd said it was important knowing that things were okay between them, but she wanted so much more, especially in light of what Logan had told her the night before.

"Patience, girl, patience," she warned herself and went back to work.

* * * * *

Hayley shut the television off and stretched. It was eleven-thirty and the news broadcast had just ended. She was debating whether to try writing a new scene she had in mind for her next book or to just call it a day when the phone rang. She picked up the portable phone. The number on the caller ID was unfamiliar but she answered it anyway.

"Hello?"

"Hayley?"

"Jace! Hi."

"Hi. I didn't wake you did I, sweetheart?"

"Nope. I just shut the television off. I was sitting here trying to decide if I wanted to work a little more or go to bed."

"How about you talk to me for a bit instead?"

"I think I could do that," Hayley teased with a pleased smile curving her lips. "So how are things going?"

"Pretty good, now that I've got the customer and his wife to agree on a few things. It's kind of hard to stay on track when they're pulling in two different directions. Especially when they want to alter the plans midstream."

"Oh dear, that doesn't sound good."

"Believe me, it's not. When the work progresses to a certain point, some changes just aren't going to happen. So how are you?"

"I'm all right." Hayley leaned back on the sofa. "Working on the new book, puttering around in the yard. I planted some iris bulbs and a couple of small flowering bushes out front. The iris should look really pretty next spring."

"Not as pretty as you."

"Thank you. You really are sweet, you know that?"

"Just tellin' the truth."

"If you're trying to get on my good side, it's working. So how are *you*? You sound a little tired."

"I am a bit. I was just, uh, watching a little television myself."

The slight pause in Jace's voice stirred Hayley's curiosity. "What were you watching?"

"Oh, um, just a movie."

"Was it good?"

"Yeah, it was okay."

"*Hmm.*" It suddenly struck Hayley just what kind of movie Jace might have been watching.

"What?"

"Jace McKenna, were you watching a porn flick?"

There was a slight pause before Jace answered. "Okay, you caught me. Yeah, I was."

"I knew it," Hayley crowed. "So, I repeat. Was it good?"

"Hayley, it was porn. It wasn't exactly Oscar-worthy material."

Hayley chuckled, loving the slight embarrassment in Jace's voice. Without stopping to think about it she asked, "So did you jack off while watching it?"

The line went completely silent.

"Jace, are you still there?"

"Hold on. I think I just swallowed my tongue."

Hayley laughed out loud. "What's the matter? You're not embarrassed, are you?"

"Truthfully? Yeah! First you get me to admit to watching porn, then you want to know if I got off while watching it. Darlin', I'll say one thing for you, you're not shy."

"Is that bad?" Hayley bit her lip, worrying that maybe she'd gone too far.

"No, it's not bad at all. It's actually exciting."

"Are you sure? 'Cause I think it's kind of exciting too. I mean, picturing you watching the movie and touching yourself."

"Oh fuck," Jace murmured, his voice going husky. "Sweetheart, if I could, I'd be crawling through this damn phone line to get to you. You've got me rock-hard again. I was watching that movie 'cause I keep thinking about what you did to me in the kitchen. You made me feel *so* good. I can't get it out of my head, and just thinkin' about it has me walking around half hard all the time."

"Umm, baby. I like the sound of that," Hayley purred. "So, in the movie, did the guy have dark hair like you?"

"Yeah, why?"

"And the girl? Was she blonde?"

"Yeah."

"Did you imagine she was me, that he was fucking me?"

"Hell no! I imagined *I* was fucking you. No one else touches you, Hayley. Ever. Not even in a fantasy," Jace growled.

His intensity sent a shiver down Hayley's spine and shaft of lust straight to her already moistening pussy. "You know, you have quite a possessive streak. It's very sexy. It makes me feel like you really want me."

"Oh, darlin', I *do* want you. And not just for sex. Haven't I made that clear?"

"Well, yeah, but maybe I'm a little insecure about it. Nobody's ever made me feel the way you do," Hayley confessed.

"Hayley, sweetheart, you've got nothin' to be insecure about. In case you haven't figured it out, you got me wrapped around your little finger."

"Jace." Hayley bit her lip, touched at Jace's admission. "Baby, I don't want you wrapped around my finger. I just want you wrapped around me."

"Oh now *that* I can do. As soon as I get home, yeah?"

"Yeah, but in the meantime, since you got me all fired up, I think it's only fair you do something about it."

"*I* got *you* fired up? Shouldn't that be the other way around?"

"Wellll, maybe," Hayley drawled. "But anyway, would you do something for me?"

"What?"

"Come for me."

"Oh fuck."

"What?"

"There went my tongue again."

97

Hayley's laugh was soft and sensual. "Is that a yes or a no?"

"It depends."

"On what?"

"On whether or not you're gonna get naked and play with that sweet little pussy of yours for me."

"Whoa," Hayley breathed. "This swallowing of the tongue thing is becoming contagious."

This time it was Jace's turn to laugh. "Two can play this game, you know. In fact, a game like this absolutely requires two."

"I can totally see that. Um, just let me get ready."

"What are you doing?"

"I'm going to the bedroom and get naked. If we're going play I want to be comfortable."

"Mmm, I like the thought of you in bed, especially a naked you in bed. We'll match."

"So are you telling me you're in bed, naked?"

"Oh yeah."

"Ummm, that's so not fair. You're a tease."

"*I'm* a tease? Look who's talking, Miss Butter-wouldn't-melt-in-my-mouth-but-jack-off-for-me-please."

"Hey! Butter not only *does* melt in my mouth, but as I recall, you did too."

Jace groaned. "Now *that's* not fair. You're going to pay, you know that, don't you?"

"Mmm, I hope so, but wait. Don't tell me how yet. I'm trying to get my clothes off."

Hayley chuckled at the sound of another groan, set the phone down and quickly stripped. She pulled the comforter and sheet down and slid into bed. She wiggled to make herself comfortable while grabbing the phone and bringing it again to her ear.

"Okay, I'm ready."

A pregnant silence fell between them. Having reached this stage, Hayley wasn't sure how to proceed. Up to now they'd been teasing each other, but not in a particularly sensual way. She shifted a little, not sure what to say next.

"Are you gettin' nervous on me, sweetheart?"

Hayley started. "Why do you ask?"

"You got awfully quiet all of a sudden."

"Well, you know…it's not like I do this kind of thing a lot."

"Same here. I'm kind of disappointed."

Hayley's stomach dropped. "Why?" she asked carefully. *He must be hating this. Why did I suggest we do such a stupid thing? Now he thinks I'm an idiot.*

"I don't get to ask you what you're wearing."

A relieved smile curved Hayley's lips. "You dope."

"Hey! That's the way it happens in movies."

"I hear you. So does that throw the whole thing off?"

"Nah, I think we can work past it. In fact," Jace's voice dropped, "do me a favor?"

"What?"

"Just relax and don't say anything for a bit. I want you to close your eyes and just breathe with me." Hayley shivered at the husky timbre of his voice. "Think about how I'm lying here wanting you so much I ache with it and if you feel like touching yourself, go ahead and do it. I am."

Silence fell between them. Hayley closed her eyes and relaxed. An image of Jace, sprawled naked across crisp white sheets, filled her mind. Her lips parted, her free hand landing gently on her torso. She moved it in slow circles, caressing her skin, shivering at the gentle friction.

In her mind's eye she could see Jace doing something very similar and suddenly staying quiet became too much.

"When I first saw you, all I could think about was how handsome you were and how much you were pissing me off by licking that damned spoon. I wanted to be the one you were licking." A quiver ran over Hayley's skin at her bold admission.

"You think I didn't want the same? When you walked in that door I was stunned. You were so beautiful. I was leaning on the counter to keep from dropping to my knees. I wanted you so much. Right then, right there."

"I've dreamed about touching you, about sliding my hands over your skin. Please do it for me, Jace. Baby, please." The sudden need was so crushing Hayley could barely breathe.

"I am, Hayley, I am."

"Where? What are you touching?"

"My hands are on my abs. I'm just lightly rubbing my skin."

"Move up. Touch one of your nipples." Hayley's body tightened at the sound of Jace's barely audible moan. "Do you like that?"

"Oh yeah."

"Is your nipple hard?"

"Mmm-hmm."

"If I was there with you, I'd lick it, suck it. It felt so good when it was hard against my tongue. I love that your nipples are sensitive like mine. I love to see the changes in your body when I touch you. See and feel your nipples get hard." Hayley panted. "I want to watch your cock go from soft to hard. I want to feel it grow in my hand. That's so amazing, so beautiful."

"Cocks aren't beautiful, darlin'," Jace gasped.

"Oh they are from this side of the fence, baby, and yours is gorgeous. And it tastes *so* good. Your pre-cum is sweet, did you know that? When you shot in my mouth the taste was mild, just a hint of bitter and salt—and I loved it. Loved the way you felt in my mouth. I can't explain how good it feels to touch you with my lips and my tongue while I take you in. The skin on your cock is so soft, like velvet or satin. It's such a contrast to what lies beneath. All that iron-hard strength and heat. When I hold you in my mouth I can feel your heartbeat against my tongue. Touch your cock for me, Jace."

Jace's groan made Hayley's stomach clench. All the time she was talking her hand was wandering over her body. Exploring fingers climbed the slope of one breast and gently squeezed. Her moan drifted across the miles that separated them.

"What are you doing, Hayley? Talk to me, sweetheart."

"I'm touching my breast. Imagining it's you touching me. Did you know that I love the way you smell? When I had you in the kitchen, when I took you in my mouth, I could smell you. The scent of your skin, that tart musk you exude when you're excited. When we're finally in bed together, I'm going to spend an hour just breathing that scent while I suck and lick your balls."

"Fuck! You're killin' me here, darlin'."

"Just making you feel good like I know you'll do for me when we're together. I want you so badly. I want to feel your breath on my skin. I want to feel your heat and the weight of you pushing me into the mattress when you fuck me. I need your hands and your mouth on me." Hayley twisted on the mattress, her need growing.

"Soon, I promise, darlin', soon. But for now, this, just this. Listen to me. Slide your hand down to your pussy. I want you to play with the hair there. Just tickle your fingers through it."

Hayley obeyed, her breath coming faster. She parted her thighs but did only what Jace asked. A cold shiver slid down her spine.

"How does it feel?"

"It tickles. *More.* Make me do more."

Jace's chuckle was strained. "Spread your legs for me. Now listen carefully. I want you to spread those plump pussy lips open and with just the tip of one finger touch yourself right where my cock would be sliding in if I was there with you. Are you wet?"

"Yesss, so wet."

"That's good, sweetheart, so good. Take your fingertip and rub all around and over your entrance. Just there, nowhere else yet."

"Mmmm, Jace, it feels good."

"I hoped you'd like that. Now slide your fingertip up and touch your clit. Just like you do when you want to make yourself come. Play with your clit for a little then back to your entrance. Just back and forth for me, sweetheart. Do you like that?"

Hayley writhed on the bed, her back arching, her hand busy between her thighs. Having Jace direct her movements was wildly exciting, the feelings caused by her own touch exquisite. The pleasure was growing, her inner thighs tensing as she spread wider. "*Yesss.* Jace, are you touching your cock? Are you stroking it?"

"Yeah, I am. It feels incredible."

"I remember how it feels, how it tastes."

"*I'm* going to be tasting soon. With my face buried between your thighs. My tongue's going to be doing just what your fingers are doing now. And while I do that I'm going to slide my fingers into your pussy and fuck you. Would you like that?"

"Yes, *please.* I want you to fuck me with your fingers and your tongue and your cock. Want your cock in me now. Oh God, Jace. It's so good, feels so good. I'm gonna come."

"That's it, sweetheart. Come with me. *Oh fuck!*"

Jace's low-pitched, guttural growl hit Hayley like a punch. She wailed with the force of the pleasure that spiked hard and fast. Radiating shock waves rippled through her body and she rode them, her hips bouncing, her heels digging into the mattress. One peak, a second and a third wrenched free every bit of sensation her body was capable of producing. It seemed to go on forever. Awareness was a thing of the past, a distant memory that held no sway over the shattering release that swept through her.

Eventually, inevitably, it returned, the enveloping cloud of bliss slowly dissipating. Hayley became aware of the fact that she was still panting, albeit more slowly. It accompanied the small, raspy whimpers that still issued from her dry throat. Her body felt completely relaxed yet strangely energized, as though every pore was hyperaware of the very air that touched it.

She took a long shuddering breath. "Thank God for multiple orgasms."

Jace's sated chuckled rumbled in her ear. She smiled at the sound and added a soft laugh of her own.

"Does that mean I don't have to ask if it was good?"

"Get real."

Jace snorted a short laugh. "You wanna ask me?"

A lazy smile curved her lips. "Was it good for you, baby?"

"Oh yeah. So good I'm wearing it up to my chin."

"Tease. You know I'd want to taste if I was there."

"Want me to taste for you?"

Hayley's mouth opened, tongue licking over her lips. "Yes." She waited a moment then heard Jace's reaction.

"Mmm, just like you said. A little bitter, a little salt."

The thought of Jace licking warm milky seed from his fingers made Hayley squirm. "How much longer are you going to be away?"

"A couple of days."

"Convince me a couple of days isn't long."

"I don't believe I can. I'm thinkin' a couple of days is a damn long time until I see you again."

"Guess we'll survive, huh?"

"Have to, darlin', I gotta see this job through."

"Hey, I know. I wouldn't expect anything less from you." Hayley stretched and yawned. "Umm, baby, you wore me out."

"Same here. You ready to go to sleep?"

"Mmm-hmm."

"Wrap yourself up tight in those blankets and pretend it's me holding you. Before you know it, it will be."

"I will, I… Good night, Jace."

"'Night, sweetheart."

Hayley hung up the phone and bit her lip. She'd come damn close to saying I love you.

* * * * *

The next two days were the longest Hayley had ever faced. She wavered between wanting Jace back so bad it hurt, and practically gibbering with nerves at the thought of being with him for real. Jace had called several times, quick calls just to say hello and tell her how his work was progressing. There was no repeat of the phone sex.

It seemed both of them were taking a step back. Jace was being quite circumspect in his conversation. Back to his usual teasing self, he made clear his affection for her, but there were no declarations of love, which made Hayley extremely glad she hadn't blurted it out herself. As much as she wanted to, it just wasn't time.

Having spent the day at the library, Hayley had worked herself into a bad mood when the one book she'd especially wanted for research was unavailable. She'd phoned the library in the nearby town of Hibberd and found out that they had the book and would hold it for her. Planning an early night in order to get up early to make the trip, she decided to stop and pick up Chinese takeout on her way home.

After getting home, she settled in and ate in front of the television, watching a wildlife documentary. At one point she found herself staring at the screen with rapt fascination as a pack of wolves took down an old stag. Instead of being horrified, she felt her muscles tighten with an odd, unreasoning need to be there. The sight of the pack feeding after the kill made her mouth water. She looked at the carton of chicken chow mein with a bit less enthusiasm. The sudden urge to have a nice, rare steak made her stomach rumble.

Hayley shook her head and frowned. She switched the channel to some comedy show and polished off her meal in a less carnal frame of mind. When she finished, she threw out the cartons and checked the front door and then the back to make sure they were locked.

Her brows beetled with concern when the back door wouldn't stay locked. The position of the locking mechanism indicated it should work, but when she pulled on the door, it opened without a hitch. She dug her phone book out of her desk and sat down to find a locksmith. She dialed the number. There was no answer, something that didn't surprise her, as late as it was.

Sighing with annoyance, she dialed Logan and Bryn's number, hoping they might know someone who could come and fix the lock. Bryn answered. "Hey, sis, it's me," Hayley said, having trouble keeping the irritation out of her voice.

"What's wrong?"

"The lock on the back door is broken and I can't find a locksmith who's open."

"Well, that's not good."

"No kidding. I suppose I could just jam a chair under the doorknob."

"Like you did when Mom and Dad left us alone that first time?"

Hayley snorted. "You're never going to let me forget that, are you?"

"Nope. But don't worry about it. I won't tell anyone you're a chicken."

"Gee, thanks. I don't suppose you know of anyone who could come to fix it tonight?"

"This is your lucky day, little sis. It just so happens I know a guy who's an expert with those kind of things. I'll send him right over."

"Oh wow, that's great! Thanks, Bryn. I owe you big time."

"I'll settle for lunch at O'Neils."

"You got it."

They said their goodbyes and Hayley settled in to wait for her rescuer. It wasn't long before there was the sound of a vehicle in the drive. She looked out the window and was surprised, then hurt and angry to see Jace. She wondered why he hadn't told her he was back in town. She walked to the door at the sound of his knock, preparing for battle. Opening it, she found him standing there with a grin on his face, looking smug, cocky and oh-so yummy. The man had everything a woman could want, at least at face value. *And doesn't he know it*, she thought.

"I hear you need me." His words implied so much more than her need to have the lock fixed.

"I *need* a locksmith. I do not need *you* but since you're here, I want you—"

"Ah, well, *want* is just as good as need. Maybe even better."

Hayley gave him a gimlet-eyed stare. "Stop interrupting me. I would *like* for you to fix the lock on the back door."

Jace smiled at her change of words. He walked in the door, deliberately not giving her time to move, so that he could brush his body against hers. "What's wrong with the lock?" he asked gruffly. Her touch caused his insides to clench tight and her scent swept into his nostrils, a cloud of ambrosia that left him ravenous.

"If I knew, I would have fixed it myself."

He noticed the delicate flush that infused her cheeks and heard the slightly breathless tone of her voice. Inevitably, his cock began to thicken. Without preliminaries he took her in his arms and softly kissed her. "Why are you angry, sweetheart?" he murmured lightly.

"When did you get back?" she asked and Jace could hear the tiniest hint of hurt in her voice.

"About an hour ago. I had some things to discuss with Logan and then I was coming right over here to surprise you. I was there when you called Bryn and told her about the back door." Jace gently rubbed her back. "You don't think I'd come back in town and not let you know, do you?"

Hayley shrugged and Jace set her back from him, firmly taking her chin in his hand. "Do you?" he asked again, searching her eyes.

"No," she answered sheepishly.

"Damn right. Now let's get this lock fixed. I have some things I want to talk to you about."

Feeling restless and edgy, he moved away and walked through the living room on his way to the kitchen. Hayley followed and almost bumped into him when he abruptly halted.

A scent assaulted his nostrils and they flared wide as his baser instincts came charging to the fore. He recognized the sour aroma of the man who'd accosted Bryn and Hayley at Morgan's. A surge of fury and incredulity hit like a bolt of lightening.

"What the hell was that man doing here?" his question was flat and accusing as he turned to face her.

Hayley felt a shiver slide down the length of her spine at the furious and possessive glow in his eyes. She felt an answering flare of aggression suffuse her being. "What man? If this is your idea of a joke, it's not funny."

Jace stepped closer. "It's no joke. What was he doing here, Hayley?"

She frowned at the deadly serious tone of his voice and felt her own ire dampen. "Jace, I'm telling you the truth. No one's been in the house but you. What makes you think someone else has been here?"

He blinked at the sincerity and puzzlement in her voice. She really didn't know. "I smell him."

Her brow rose and she took a deep breath. Astonishment caused her eyes to widen. "I smell him too. Why didn't I notice it before? I thought you were joking."

"I'm dead serious," he answered and walked out to the kitchen to examine the door lock. "As to why you didn't notice it, maybe the smell of your Chinese food masked it." A frisson of alarm then stone-cold rage swept through him. "This lock has been tampered with. How did you know it wasn't working? It looks fine."

Hayley moved to stand beside him. "I always pull on the door after I lock it." She looked uncomfortable for a moment then decided to share the memory with him that Bryn had teased her with. "When I was in my mid-teens, our parents went away for the weekend. It was the first time they left us on our own and of course I was thrilled, at least on the surface. I didn't tell Bryn, but I felt kind of uneasy about it." She shrugged.

"Mom and Dad were my security and they weren't there for the first time I could remember. I had a bad dream the first night they were gone. I dreamt that I locked the front door, but it kept swinging open. Something bad was coming. No matter how many times I locked it, it wouldn't stay shut." She gave him a wry grin. "I woke up and couldn't sleep, so I wedged a chair under the front door. I went back to bed and slept like a log. Anyway, I got in the habit of always pulling on the door after I lock it, and this time it just came right open. What makes you think it's been tampered with?"

"These scratches, there are tool marks here. Someone fixed this lock to make sure it looked functional but wouldn't work." He looked at Hayley, concern clearly apparent in his eyes. "Are you sure no one's been through your things? Are you missing anything?"

Surprised and somewhat alarmed, Hayley looked at Jace, her guard totally down, an uneasy vulnerability clearly visible in her eyes. "I didn't notice anything. If someone was in the house they didn't disturb anything."

Seeing the concern in her eyes, Jace felt his protective instincts kick into high gear. He looked at his watch. "The hardware store is closed. I won't be able to get the things I need to fix this until tomorrow, which means one of two things. Either you come home with me tonight, or I'm staying here."

"I'm not going home with you! I'm staying right here," she answered defiantly, not liking the idea of being driven out of her own home. "Who knows what they'd do with no one here."

"Fine with me, the couch looks comfy." Jace moved into Hayley's space. "Much as I want to, I won't share a bed with you. Not under these circumstances. If that guy shows up I want to catch him, and you're just too damned distracting." He leaned down and pressed a soft kiss to her lips.

Hayley's stomach clenched and she felt a thumping pulse ripple through her pussy in answer to his touch and sweet admission. She might have said nothing, but stubborn pride had her wanting to make sure he didn't take too much for granted. She stepped back, unconsciously licking her lips. Jace's taste had her almost changing her mind but she held her ground.

"I don't remember asking you to share my bed," she told him with a haughty lift of her chin. She found herself torn at the prospect. The idea of Jace in her bed brought back thoughts of the other night and what they'd shared on the phone. Even before that night she'd had dreams of decadent seduction and writhing bodies in which Jace played a starring role. Just thinking about it had her breaking out in a sweat.

Jace still hadn't mentioned the L-word and Hayley wasn't anxious to begin another relationship that would end up going nowhere. This thing with Jace was too important to take lightly. There were already too many unanswered questions pending. Seesawing between what her head told her, what her heart wanted and what her body demanded had Hayley's head whirling.

The teasing smile left Jace's face, his expression suddenly serious. "I think that's a question we're going to be addressing real soon, but for now, someone broke the lock on your door. I say it's the guy who threatened you. Whether you believe me or not, the point is, this person didn't do it to steal anything. That leads me to believe that what he really wants is to take you by surprise sometime when you're here alone." He looked deeply into Hayley's blue eyes. "If you think I'm going to stand by and let that happen, think again. And if you have even the slightest notion of telling me I don't need to stay, save your breath. I'm not leaving you here alone."

She felt a warm wave of affection sweep through her. Jace really did care and she couldn't help but be pleased by the thought. "I'll get you a pillow and a blanket," she answered, giving in gracefully.

Jace smiled. "Good, I was hoping you'd say that. I don't want to fight with you, I just want to be here when that bastard comes back." He opened the door and stepped out on the back porch. "I'm going to put my truck in the garage so anyone cruising by will think you're alone."

"Get that idea from all your amorous adventures with the ladies of Whispering Springs?"

"A gentleman never tells," he answered and gave her an impudent grin.

With an annoyed frown on her face, Hayley watched him walk out to the drive then turned back to the kitchen. She felt a tightness in her chest and admitted the truth to herself, finally and completely accepting the finality of it. She was in love with Jace McKenna.

The thought of him being with someone else was disturbing. She knew whatever he did before they met was his business, just as he could say nothing about the fact that she'd had an encounter or two in her own past. Shrugging in resignation, she walked through the living room and down the hall to her bedroom. Once there, she dug out an extra pillow and blanket for his overnight vigil.

* * * * *

Jace couldn't sleep. In order to trap a possible intruder, they'd decided to go to bed early and turn the lights out. After several uneventful hours, Jace was still wide awake. There was nothing wrong with the sofa. It was fairly comfortable as those things go, and plenty long enough that he could stretch out. With things so quiet, he'd even stripped out of his clothes, nude being his usual style of sleepwear. He'd hesitated at first, thinking he should keep his clothes on, then shrugged. *With clothes or without, I can catch the guy just as easily, and if I need to change in a hurry, I won't have to worry about getting undressed.*

The problem was, the light blanket and pillow Hayley had given him were redolent with her scent. It was driving him insane. His cock hadn't softened the least bit since he'd first stretched out. Instead of resting, it stood tall and solidly proud, declaring its readiness to the world. It was insisting it was going to stay fully erect until relief was offered.

It didn't help that he could hear Hayley moving around in her bedroom. The first thing that really caught his attention was when she went in to her connecting bathroom. He heard the shower running. The thought of her totally nude, with the water cascading over her satiny skin, brought back memories of that first moonlit night that he'd seen her swimming in the pond. Thinking of her now in the shower, he groaned when he pictured her hands roving over her body as she soaped herself. He could clearly see her lush, full breasts, slick and foamy with the slippery suds. His imagination followed the path of her hands as they moved down her torso, over her belly and lower still. Jace's lips parted, his breath coming faster as he pictured her hands sliding between her thighs. She would caress her pussy and languidly take her time at the chore.

His imagination went into overdrive as he pictured her pleasuring herself, her soap-slick fingers rubbing her clit and sliding into her sheath to be met by the warm cream of her own lubrication. Jace was breathing hard and squirming when he was suddenly brought back to reality by the sound of Hayley getting into bed. Without skipping a beat, his imagination changed venues and again Hayley was pleasuring herself. This time she was laid out on her bed, her thighs spread wide as her fingers expertly worked all her pleasure points with practiced ease.

The fact that she was restless only helped his imagination. Each time she moved he could easily pretend that she was squirming from the pleasure she was experiencing in the imaginary masturbation scene he'd placed her in.

On a muttered oath, Jace threw the blanket back, sat up and swung his feet to the floor. Leaning back, he looked down the length of his body and silently contemplated the thick, hard length of his cock as it returned his look with a one-eyed glare. Giving in to the inevitable, he wrapped his fingers around the base and squeezed then slid his hand up to the reddened, plum-shaped head.

* * * * *

Down the hall, Hayley was having a similar problem. Even sternly reminding herself that she had to get up early to make the trip to Hibberd's library for the book she needed didn't help. She'd taken a hot shower, hoping to relax, but she still felt tense and *needy*. She kept changing positions, trying to find that just—right—feeling that would help her drift off to sleep, but she never found it. Her normally comfortable bed had suddenly become hostile and unwelcoming.

She knew what was bothering her. The fact that Jace was only a few rooms away and probably at least half naked. The thought made her roll over into a new position. She stared with unseeing eyes at the ceiling. She'd already pictured him taking off his shirt before lying down, and it made her breathless.

On the verge of giving in to the wicked thoughts that were filling her head, Hayley heard a sound and froze. Anxious to know if someone showed up in the night, she'd left her bedroom door open several inches. She sat up and slid out of bed, stalking silently to her door. Another muffled sound came to her straining ears and she frowned, puzzled by it. It didn't sound like any kind of a struggle, but it came to mind that maybe Jace was having a nightmare or possibly talking in his sleep.

Needing to satisfy her curiosity, she eased the door open, slipped through and carefully walked the length of the hall. She stayed close to the wall so as to be out of sight of anyone in the living room. Why, she wasn't sure, but some impulse told her to do it and she complied without question. When she reached the end of the hall, she stopped and listened for a moment, hearing the sound of deep breathing. She frowned and peeped around the edge of the wall and was barely able to keep from gasping out loud as her mouth dropped open.

Leaning casually against the back of the sofa, his legs slightly spread, not only was Jace totally naked, he was masturbating! Eyes open wide, she took in the most electrifying sight she'd ever seen as heat and instant arousal gathered at her center and melted into a pool of creamy moisture.

There were millions of handsome men in the world, but for Hayley, none more so than Jace. He had that elusive *something* that permeated every cell in her body, making her crave only him. His body was magnificent. She'd already seen the broad shoulders and muscular arms. And his chest, with its delineated pectoral muscles covered by that pelt of dark hair. Her fingers tingled with the remembered feel of his back and she longed to run them through the silky hair on his chest.

His abs were taut and chiseled, the first eight-pack she'd ever seen. They were mouthwatering and she could see herself running her tongue over the muscular hills and valleys. Rigid, masculine nipples surrounded by copper-brown areolas were plainly visible and she scrunched her eyes closed in an effort to keep from whimpering when Jace reached up to pinch one hard nub.

He moaned, a deep rolling growl that set her heart racing ever faster while she squirmed at the moisture that flooded her pussy. She'd never gotten this wet this fast before. It was pleasurable and disconcerting all at once, especially when she felt a tiny rivulet wet her inner thighs.

Pushing her attention back to Jace, her eyes followed the trail of dark hair on his chest as it moved downward, divided itself to meander around his bellybutton, then re-formed to make an enticing trail that led down to the full, dark bush at the base of his cock. Hayley had trouble breathing when she focused all her attention on his cock. Though she'd seen it before, it still took her breath away.

Thick, hard and long, the length easily came even with and went beyond his bellybutton. The fat, smooth head was copiously leaking pre-cum and gleaming softly. Under his smoothly stroking hand, she could see the plump veins that ran under the dark-reddish, satiny skin. It was the most beautiful thing she'd ever seen, and she shivered with desire at the thought of riding that magnificent shaft.

Jace was tanned a dark, golden bronze over his entire body. The sprinkling of dark hair on his legs and arms accompanied by that wonderful pelt on his chest made Hayley want to rub herself over him like a cat in heat. He seemed at ease, resting against the back of the sofa, eyes closed. His free hand came up to slowly rub over his torso, and again he pinched the tight bud of one nipple while his other hand slowly stroked the entire length of his cock.

As his fist came back up, he would linger at the upper third of his erection. His hand would tighten as he used a short twisting stroke that caused his muscles to grow taut, his hips to push upward and his breath to come even faster while fresh drops of pre-cum leaked from the slit in the plump head. Those clear, crystal drops reflected what light was available and slid down over the head, leaving a fresh trail of moisture. Mouth open, he would momentarily press his lips together, then his tongue would come out to slide sensuously over his full bottom lip.

Every move he made had Hayley near to groaning aloud, especially when another husky groan came rumbling up from the depths of his chest. It was then she realized it was Jace's groans of pleasure that had drawn her to the living room. *And thank God I was awake to hear it!* she thought. Her admiring gaze took in the rest of his body, his thighs, calves and feet. She couldn't help but marvel at his feet. Long and elegant, they were classically beautiful, as though shaped by a master sculptor.

He continued the repetitive movement of his hand and moments later, his entire body seemed to tighten, his muscles bunching and flexing. She watched as the rhythm of his stroking fingers increased over the thick, throbbing column in his fist. They moved faster and faster, their touch concentrating more and more on the upper portion of his cock. The rate of his breathing increased and a feral growl was torn from his throat.

Hayley was breathing with him and swore his cock swelled even larger moments before it blasted a thick, white rope of semen that leapt out to land with a splash on his torso. Several more spurts flew from the flaring tip until his chest and belly were decorated with lines and dots of warm and fragrant male seed. Jace's body slowly relaxed and he heaved what sounded like a contented sigh.

Hayley's own breathing was still elevated, rushing in and out of her lungs, especially now that she realized that Jace had nothing to distract him. She was going to have to be doubly careful sneaking back to her bedroom. Before she was able to take the first step, Jace spoke out loud and she jumped.

"Did you like watching me, Hayley?"

She gasped softly, her face going instantly red with mortification at being caught. *Oh shit!* "I'm sorry," she stuttered aloud, and stepping forward, she shivered under the weight of his heated regard. "I heard a noise. I really didn't mean to spy on you."

"Don't be sorry, I'm glad you were watching. It made it much more exciting," Jace confessed as he ran the tapered tip of one long finger through the warm semen that painted his body. He scooped some up and brought his finger to his lips, his tongue coming out to lave over the tip before he sucked the finger inside.

Mouth open, tongue almost twitching with the desire to emulate him, Hayley watched in rapt fascination.

"Want some?" he asked huskily.

Hayley nodded, not about to deny the truth, but she wanted an answer to a question first. "You knew I was watching?"

"I heard you sneaking down the hallway."

"Why didn't you stop?"

"I didn't want to, but you still haven't answered *my* first question. Did you like watching me?"

The expression in Jace's eyes was compelling, their bright glow making Hayley shiver once again. She shifted, her body's reaction growing unbearable. Innate honesty prevented her from lying. "Yes. I liked watching you. Very much."

Jace reached out his hand to her. "Come here, baby."

His voice was so deep and soft, gentle, yet commanding. She found herself walking toward him, her own hand reaching for his. Their fingers touched, palms slid together and fingers gripped. Jace urged her down on his lap. Lost in a fog of growing desire and overwhelming hunger, Hayley willingly let him guide her. His free hand found her face and he brought his mouth to hers, pulling a moan from her open lips.

Never one to pass up an opportunity, Jace smoothly slid his tongue into her mouth and issued his own groan as her taste exploded inside his mouth with a force that left him dizzy.

He explored and Hayley answered his need with her own until their tongues were actively dueling. His hand slid from her face over her throat and down to cup a full warm breast. The nipple beaded to a hard point that poked impudently into the palm of his hand as he gently squeezed. Hayley gasped into his mouth, squirmed in his lap and pressed tighter against his exploring fingers.

Leaving the temptation of her breast, he moved over her abdomen and down the length of her thigh until he found the hem of her t-shirt. His fingers slid underneath. The heat of her skin burned against his hand and he was drawn irresistibly upward, seeking her fevered core.

Lost in his kisses and the sensual exploration of his hands, Hayley came to with a jolt at the feel of his hand inches from her flooding pussy. "Jace," she whispered, covering his hand and holding it still against her thigh, staring at him with eyes filled with uncertainty.

"You need," he growled softly. "Let me give."

Hayley looked deep into the glow of his eyes. It all seemed so simple, need and want and give and take. A shudder of desire ran through her and she nodded, releasing his hand. She did need, oh-so badly and he was the only one she wanted to assuage that aching need with.

"Open for me, sweetheart, this is going to be *sooo* good."

She spread her thighs and moaned deep in her throat as Jace wasted no time in wedging his hand between them. She hadn't donned the shorts that matched her sleep shirt. There was nothing to impede his progress. His long fingers petted the drenched pelt that guarded her mound and he uttered a wordless growl that set Hayley on fire. Parting the swollen lips of her pussy, a slick finger probed and slid deep into her weeping slit.

She gasped and tightened her muscles, holding the invader deep inside. In spite of the tight grip, Jace easily worked his finger in and out of the slick, warm heat that filled her grasping channel and very quickly sent a second finger to join the first, easing her open.

"Jace," Hayley groaned, panting as ripples of pleasure assailed her senses.

Jace withdrew his fingers and gently shushed her whimper of disappointment. He lifted his fingers, wet with her fragrant dew, and drew them into his mouth, tasting her. Hayley watched wide-eyed, and shivered at the inferno that built in his eyes.

"So sweet," he growled. "You taste so sweet. Honey and heat, passion and desire. All in one wild, sweet nectar. One day soon I'm going to *feast* between your thighs," he promised as he slid his hand back into position, his fingers once again penetrating the depths of her quivering pussy. "But for now, just this and this," he whispered as his thumb found her clit.

Hayley stiffened and shuddered, her breath hard and fast as Jace expertly played a passionate game between her willing thighs. "Please, please, please, I *need...*" she gasped and writhed against him.

"Need what? This?" he questioned, pressing himself against her, his cock once more full and hard.

"Yes!" Hayley admitted and broke free of his restraining grasp.

She scrambled to change positions until she was straddling his lap and impatiently tore her sleep shirt over her head, throwing it out and away from them. Reaching out, her fingers wrapped around his swollen length. Jace threw his head back, groaning as she slowly stroked him. Her need rode her hard. She rose up on her knees, holding him steady while she lowered herself to him.

"Wait! Hayley, baby, wait," Jace groaned.

"Nooo," she wailed and writhed against him.

"Condom. We need a condom."

"No, we don't. I'm on the pill," she gasped.

Instantly, Jace's hand appeared by her own and she released his cock, both her hands going to his shoulders. She let him guide his cock in and held on as the plump head softly nestled against her entrance and began its journey deep inside. She circled her hips, spreading her moisture while pushing down, and gasped as the hot, throbbing head popped inside. Once begun, the rest of his shaft easily followed as she lowered herself to his lap.

She felt her muscles part, the rich friction of his body sending euphoric shivers down her spine. Both of them were breathing heavily and she felt a heated puff of air moments before his hot mouth engulfed her breast and began earnestly suckling her pointed nipple.

Hayley whimpered with pleasure. Her hips undulated against him as she stimulated her sheath and swollen clit with short thrusts. His cock head hit her cervix, sending ever increasing jolts of bliss through her, and she ground against it, groaning at the sensation. Jace let her move as she wished for a time, then emitted a frustrated growl at her efforts. She felt his hands grasp the cheeks of her buttocks. Holding her tightly to him, he stood effortlessly. Hayley wrapped her long legs around his body and held on as he walked a few short feet.

She bounced against him with the movement. "Jace, please," she pleaded until suddenly her back came in contact with the wall.

In a voice husky with desire, he murmured in her ear. "This is more like it. Hard and fast, darlin'. Let's *fuck*."

He withdrew and she waited for his return, but Jace had stopped. Digging her nails into the hard muscles of his shoulders, she did her best to shake him with little result. "Now, damn it, now!" she demanded, tightening her thighs around his hips.

Jace gave her a feral grin and complied, sliding in to the hilt with a force and power that swept her breath away and tore a gasping groan from her throat. Hayley was unable to do more than hold on as he thrust again and again, long, hard strokes that sent his thick cock surging in and out until she felt she would go mad with the pleasure.

Sweat broke out on their skin. Heated air swirled around them, saturated with scents that mingled and became a drugging cocktail of male-female arousal. The sweet-spicy musk perfumed the air, screaming of need and encouraging their wanton desire for a pure, abandoned mating.

Hayley was lost and blind in a fog of sensation, filled with smooth skin and hard muscle, rough hair that abraded her nipples, trickles of sweat and the juices between her thighs that emitted a slurping sound with every thrust of Jace's thick, battering cock. Their grunts and moans of effort and pleasure rang out, accompanied by the thumping slap of their bodies as they slammed together. The heady scent of sex wrapped its tendrils around them, tying them with invisible bonds.

Arms around his shoulders and overwhelmed by the pleasure that was rapidly building to an explosion, she fastened her teeth in Jace's skin and bit. He froze for a split second and uttered a deep rolling growl that quickly became a short intense howl of sound that caused the hair on Hayley's arms to stand up. At the same time, it sent a bolt of wild desire through her that twisted her gut with a sensation near pain.

Jace reacted with savage intensity, his thrusts becoming short, hard staccato jabs that quickly had Hayley sobbing for release as the pressure built unbearably higher and higher. He moved with an endless, fluid rhythm that sent her crashing over the edge with a wailing cry. Her pussy gripped and released him in rapid-fire pulses, milking the thick, solid length of him until, with a guttural roar, he exploded and emptied himself within her. Long, hard spurts were felt as pulsing shudders within Hayley's clasping channel. The added cream of his release sluiced between them until their pubic hair was matted with warm, milky semen and the sweet cream of Hayley's arousal.

Jace managed to stagger back to the sofa and landed with enough accuracy that he kept them from the floor and left them sprawled together in an exhausted heap. Hayley rested with boneless grace on top of him. Both were struggling to regain their breath, and several minutes went by as they did just that. Strength slowly returned to well-exercised limbs and Jace began to gently stroke his hand over the creamy smooth skin of her back.

Outside, though it was still mostly dark, the first promise of daylight was emerging from below the horizon. A few sleepy chirps sounded from the trees that shaded the house.

Hayley began to shake in his arms. Jace's initial alarm changed to understanding when he heard her satisfied chuckle. He tightened his arms around her, nuzzling his face in her hair. "Happy?" he asked.

She attempted a nod. "More than happy."

His body had tensed under her and Hayley rose up at the taut bunching of his muscles. She looked at him, love clearly showing in her eyes.

"Your eyes are glowing," she told him, seeing satisfaction and pure joy reflected there.

"So are yours," he answered softly.

Hayley frowned, a confused smile on her face. "What do you mean?"

Chapter Eight

ഇ

Jace opened his mouth to explain and froze, his head cocked as though listening. Determined to know what secrets he was keeping from her, Hayley didn't stop to think about why he was there in the first place, but lifted herself off him and demanded, "What do you mean? How can my eyes be glowing? I don't have your medical condition, whatever it is. Which reminds me. You said you'd explain that to me."

"I will, just not right this minute," Jace replied in a distracted tone. "What I meant to say was, um, you're glowing. You know, like afterglow. Now, hush a minute."

Hayley narrowed her eyes. How dare he tell her to hush! Something was wrong definitely wrong here. Jace was obviously trying to cover up what he'd originally said, but at the same time he didn't seem to be putting much effort into it. He wasn't looking at her and he seemed preoccupied by something.

She was just about to question him again when Jace cursed and eased her aside. Coming up off the sofa, he ran for the back door. Hayley stared after him in blank surprise until a sudden realization hit her. Grabbing her t-shirt off the floor, she ran after him. Jace was already gone from sight. She was standing on the porch, listening for any sound that would give her a clue as to which direction he'd gone, when a shot rang out. Hayley gasped and felt her heart stop.

"Jace," she blurted out in a stricken whisper and scrambled for the phone in the kitchen, quickly dialing 9-1-1.

After explaining the situation to the operator and giving her address, she hung up and grabbed the flashlight she'd placed in the corner of the kitchen counter for emergencies.

Heedless of the way she was dressed, she was determined to find Jace. She crossed the porch and headed across the backyard when she was brought up short by the sound of his voice calling to her.

She turned to find him coming toward her from around the side of the house and ran to meet him, throwing herself in his arms. "Are you all right?" she questioned anxiously, her voice taut with anxiety.

"Fine," he replied shortly in disgust. "He got away. The bastard had someone waiting with a car. I didn't even get the license plate."

"I called 9-1-1. I heard the shot and I was afraid…I was afraid that you…"

Jace hugged her tightly. "I'm okay, baby, everything's okay. That's why I didn't catch him. I had to dive into the hedge to keep from getting shot."

His voice was so filled with disgust that Hayley was surprised by a nervous laugh of relief. He gave her another hard hug. "Let's get some clothes on. I don't want to talk to the sheriff with my goodies hanging out."

By the time the sheriff arrived, took their statements and departed, the sun was well up. They were exhausted. Jace refused to leave her alone, despite the fact that there was little chance the would-be assailant would return any time soon. At this point Hayley saw little reason to keep him on the sofa, so she dragged him to her bed. He protested that he needed to fix the lock, but Hayley insisted he get some sleep. Once in bed, there was no thought of anything but sleep. They both drifted off.

Hayley was the first to wake. It was almost noon and she found herself completely tangled up with Jace. She lay on her right side. He was spooned solidly against her back, one arm snuggled firmly under her breasts and one leg over hers with her left leg resting between his.

She smiled sleepily, warmth and affection flowing through her as she began the complicated process of unwinding herself from Jace's possessive embrace. She didn't get far. As soon as she tried to carefully pry his arm lose, his grip tightened and he nuzzled the back of her neck.

"Where do you think you're going?" he asked with a deep, husky rasp.

"To shower," she replied snuggling against him. "I have to drive to the library in Hibberd to pick up a book."

Jace began kissing the back of her neck, sending shivers down her spine. "We have a library here in town, darlin'," he murmured, his breath imparting a wispy, warm tickle.

Hayley felt her nipples tighten as Jace's cock hardened against her. "I know that, *darlin'*," she said breathlessly, emulating his endearment. "But they don't have the book I need for some research I'm doing."

"Mmm, want me to go with you?"

"To Hibberd or the shower?"

"Either, both. Could be fun either way," he murmured, finding that sensitive hollow behind her ear and sensually caressing it with his tongue.

"Mmm," Hayley moaned and shivered. "You're supposed to fix my lock."

"Guess that just leaves the shower. Come on, sweetheart," he growled, unwinding himself from around her and urging her up. "Let's see how dirty we can get before we get clean."

Hayley laughed and let him drag her into the bathroom, which was equipped with a large shower enclosed in frosted glass. There was plenty of room for two, and Jace got the water running while Hayley brushed her teeth. As soon as the temperature was adjusted to his satisfaction, he stepped out and Hayley offered him a toothbrush. She started pulling her sleep shirt off.

"Let me help you with that," Jace offered, setting the toothbrush down on the counter.

His hands moved under the hem of her shirt where it rested against her thighs and began to slide slowly up the length of her body, taking the shirt with them.

"Your skin is so soft," he commented reverently.

Hayley shivered as the tips of his thumbs brushed through her pubic hair.

"So are other things," he breathed as her shirt rose higher.

She inhaled sharply, her stomach quivering. Jace's hands continued upward. They moved over her waist and abdomen, his fingers caressing her sides while his thumbs began following the rounded path up and over her full, firm breasts. Her nipples, already taut, beaded tightly, drawing a breathy moan from her as his thumbs brushed over their sensitized tips.

"And some things are hard," he teased with a devilish twinkle in his eyes.

Hayley managed a smile and reached out to run a trembling finger up the rock-hard length of his cock. "Very hard," she agreed, her smile widening at the small growl Jace emitted.

"Lift your arms," he ordered urgently.

Hayley complied and her shirt was swept over her head. Before she was completely free of it, Jace bent and took one hard nipple into his mouth and began suckling her. Moaning at the wave of desire that swept through her, Hayley's hands cupped his head, her fingers clutching his hair.

"Jace," she moaned as his mouth and tongue diligently worked her nipple.

"Get in the shower, darlin', I'll be right there."

Smiling at her dazed condition, he turned her in the direction of the shower and gave her luscious tush a gentle pat. Hayley obeyed and Jace quickly brushed his teeth before joining her. He paused to take in the arousing sight, reminded of the first time he'd seen Hayley. She was standing under the showerhead, her body glistening and wet with the streams of water that cascaded over her.

Jace intercepted her as she reached for her bottle of shampoo. "Let me," he offered, taking the bottle and squeezing some of its contents into his hand.

As he gently massaged the shampoo into her hair and scalp, Hayley murmured her approval. "If you ever want to change careers, you could make a mint as a hairdresser. Women would come from miles around for this."

"Hairdresser! I don't think so, babe. Besides, I wouldn't do this for anyone but you."

"Aww, Jace, that's really sweet."

"Hey, I'm a sweet guy. Let's get your hair rinsed."

That done, Jace quickly shampooed and rinsed his own hair. "Now for the best part," he said, flashing her a wicked grin as he soaped his hands with shower gel. "Bring that bodacious body of yours over here, darlin'."

Hayley laughed at the way he wiggled his eyebrows at her. "You're a nut," she told him, but she moved closer all the same and hummed with pleasure as he ran his hands over her shoulders and back.

"I fantasized about this last night."

"Oh?" Hayley asked, pleased and curious.

"Actually, in my fantasy you were in the shower alone and you started pleasuring yourself." He slid his hands around to cup her breasts, tenderly kneading the sensitive globes. "You ever do that, Hayley?"

"Of course," she admitted breathlessly, leaning into his touch.

Jace's brows rose at her frank admission and he smiled mischievously. "How about you show me what you do?"

"I've got a better idea, why don't you show me your fantasy?"

"Oh yeah, I like that idea," he said, fire flaring in his eyes. "Put your hands right here."

Jace guided Hayley's hands to cup her own breasts and laid his hands on top of hers, directing her movements. Slick with soap, their hands slid slowly over the front of her body as he pressed tightly against her back. His thick erection was compressed between their bodies, lodged against the enticing crevice that separated the cheeks of her bottom. With a few swaying movements of his hips, he was able to firmly wedge his cock between them. Once there he started a slow, rocking motion that sent his cock sliding over her tender, pink rosebud.

Hayley shuddered, moaning at the unaccustomed feel. No one had ever touched her there. The wild urge to taste such a dark and sinful pleasure sluiced through her as Jace continued the sensual torment and moved their hands lower, over her curved belly and down. He urged her to widen her stance then guided their joined right hands between her thighs. Hayley arched her back when the pad of her finger slid over her clit.

"Ease your finger over the left side of your clit, babe," Jace crooned softly.

Hayley slid her finger to the left as Jace slid his to the right, effectively trapping her clit between them. With his hand over hers he kept their fingers moving in a slow, steady rhythm that sent a rush of heat and need pulsing through the swelling folds of her pussy. Her sweet cream, thick and silky, coated their fingers, the delicate, musky scent rising like a silent plea.

Hayley panted, pushing against him. "Jace, please, I'm burning up."

"I know, sweet, I know. I can feel your heat. It's like holding liquid fire in my hands, so hot, so wet. Brand me, Hayley."

Jace turned her to face the shower wall, palms flat against the tiles, while urging her to bend forward. He positioned himself between her thighs and, bending his knees, he took his demanding cock in hand, guiding it to the swollen lips of her pussy. Finding her entrance, he thrust.

Hayley moaned her pleasure and struggled to push back into him. His body and the thick spike of his erection pinned her in place. Jace rolled his hips. The movement stirred his cock within her in short, teasing, in-and-out increments.

"Mmm, Jace. You feel so good. So big and hard and hot. Fuck me, baby. Please!"

Hayley's wanton words electrified him. Jace grabbed her hips, his own pumping forward and back as his cock stroked in and out. "Is this what you want, sweetheart? Like this?"

"Yes!"

Jace rested his chin on her shoulder his mouth against her ear. "Hayley, Hayley, baby. Tell me how *this* feels." His left hand released her hip to slip between her thighs. Parting the slippery folds of her pussy, his finger found her clit and gently manipulated the swollen bud.

Hayley stiffened and shuddered against him. "*Goood*, so good, so good, so good," she moaned. "Don't stop. Make me come. Oh God, Jace, I need to come!"

"Soon, baby, soon," he promised.

Holding her tightly between his body and the shower wall, Jace released his hold on her other hip. Easing his upper body back, he slid his hand between them. He found the inviting crevice between the firm cheeks of her ass and let his fingers glide over that tempting track. Moving lower, he touched the base of his cock where it disappeared inside her body. Anointing his fingers in Hayley's pearly cream, he made the return journey through the tempting cleft of her buttocks. His finger found her tight rosebud. It convulsively clenched at his touch and Hayley whimpered, shivering against him.

"Tell me how this feels," Jace whispered as he slid his finger inside the hot velvet of her dark channel.

Hayley convulsed and bucked against him as she screamed out her release. Attacked on so many fronts, her body shattered. Not one nerve in her body was spared the blazing pleasure that burned through her. Her knees buckled. Only Jace's strength kept her on her feet as he completed the ritual, finding his own release deep inside the clenching, quivering demand of her weeping pussy.

Breathing heavily, Jace wrapped his arms around her. "Are you still with me, darlin'?"

Hayley nodded shakily, her body still riding out the aftershocks. Small moans accompanied each electrifying peak until her shudders quieted and stilled. She took a deep, shaky breath. "Jace," she whispered.

"Right here, sweetheart, right here."

They stood together quietly as the warm water continued to cascade over their bodies. Hayley turned in Jace's arms and looked up at him. Her silvery-gray eyes were aglow with warmth, liquid with unshed tears. Wordlessly she pulled free and poured soap into her hands. She washed him, worshipping his body with her touch.

Their world became a glass-enclosed cubicle filled with steam, wet warmth and unspoken love. It found its outlet in candid looks that hid nothing and touches that radiated intense feeling and tender passion. It was only the cooling of the water that finally drove them out, laughing as they escaped the cold spray.

Frolicking like carefree children, they dried, dressed and readied themselves for the day. Together they fixed breakfast and cleaned up the dishes. Finding no other reason to delay, especially as it was already nearing two o'clock, Hayley grabbed her purse and keys.

"You know how to get to Hibberd?" Jace teased.

"Yes, Mr. Smarty. I even have a map. See?" She waved it under his nose.

"If you ask me real nice, I'll show you the route with the prettiest scenery."

"All right," she agreed. Hayley circled around him, trailing her hand across his chest, around his shoulder and over his back. Placing both hands on his shoulders, she leaned against him, rubbing her breasts against his back. Her lips played over the back of his neck then found his ear. "Is this nice enough?" she whispered, before taking his earlobe in her mouth to nibble and suck.

"Mmm," he growled. "That's more than nice, darlin'. If you don't stop it, your trip's gonna be delayed."

Hayley chuckled and stepped back around him. She wrapped her arms around him and planted a soft kiss on his lips. "You asked for it, *darlin'*," she teased, then stepped back.

Jace took the map and spread it out on the table. "Here's hoping you give me everything I ask for," he murmured.

Hayley grinned and stood next to him. Jace slipped an arm around her waist while he pointed out his favorite route to Hibberd. "If you go this way, there's hills and woods *and* an old-fashioned covered bridge."

"Oh I love those. They're so picturesque."

"I'll take you to the bridge festival this fall. I have a feeling you'll really like that."

"That sounds like fun."

"All right. So here's the plan," Jace explained, and pulled her around to face him. "I'm going to fix the lock on your door and take care of some other stuff. You do whatever you need to do and we'll meet back here this evening. There are some things I need to discuss with you," he told her, his eyes solemn and sincere. "It's very important. Okay?"

With a whimsical smile on her face, Hayley nodded.

"I'm serious, Hayley."

"I didn't say you weren't."

"Stop smiling at me like that."

"Why?"

"It does funny things to my stomach."

Her smile widened into a grin. "Now you know how I feel."

"Do I make your stomach do flip-flops?" he asked with a pleased, boyish smile.

"Yeah," she admitted softly.

Jace pulled her close and held her, swaying back and forth. He sighed. "That's good to know, darlin'. That's very good to know."

Hayley relaxed against him. She could hear the smile in his voice and closed her eyes. For a few long and silent moments, they stood together, letting contentment wrap them in its warm embrace.

Finally Jace released her. He kissed her. A slow, gentle kiss, filled with unspoken words and promises. "Get going and be careful, you hear?"

"I will. You too," Hayley teased.

Seeing the sparkle in her eyes, Jace sent her a mock frown. "What's that mean?"

"It means don't smash any important body parts while I'm gone."

"Very funny. I'll remind you that smashing my thumb with the hammer was all your fault."

"I know," she admitted, giving him a look of contrition. "I'm sorry."

"No, you're not," he accused.

A small smile curved her lips. "You're right. I'm not. I was flattered."

"I'm glad you enjoyed my pain."

"Aww, poor baby. When I get home, I'll kiss it and make it all better."

"Well now," Jace answered with a leer. "That's a real nice offer, but my thumb's okay now. But I've got something else you can kiss."

Hayley grinned and raised a mocking brow. "I'll just bet you do."

She headed out the back door, laughing as she went.

"Is that a yes?" Jace called after her while following her around to the front.

"See you later," she answered, got in her car and backed down the driveway. With a wave she drove away.

Jace shook his head. Smiling he murmured to himself, "I love that woman."

He halted in his tracks. For some reason the words sent a shock through him. He'd accepted the concept of Hayley as his mate, had even told Logan that he loved her, but this was the first time he actually felt the power of the words. They melted through his being and electrified every nerve, suffusing him with excitement. He *loved* her. He felt short of breath. A wave of wonder and uncertainty swept over him. He was fairly certain she felt the same, but only until she said the words to him would he be able to still the uneasy qualms that stirred in his belly.

He looked forward to the coming evening with anticipation and dread. Tonight, no matter the consequences, he would tell Hayley that he was a werewolf. The thought brought a shudder of near panic. "Damn," he muttered. "I gotta talk to Logan."

* * * * *

Hayley made the trip to Hibberd without incident. Jace had been right. The scenery along the way was beautiful. There were woodlands and open meadows, cultivated fields and several farms that were obviously owned by Amish families. While on the road, she passed two Amish wagons, the occupants dressed in their traditional black, white and gray.

The city of Hibberd was considerably larger than Whispering Springs. Luckily, Hayley had asked the librarian for directions. She found the library with little trouble and parked her car in the smaller east lot, avoiding the large lot that bordered the main street with its heavier flow of traffic.

She pocketed her keys and grabbed her purse, not bothering to lock the car. Walking into the library, she wasn't aware of the hostile gaze that followed her.

"Do you believe the luck? That uppity bitch showing up here in Hibberd? And all alone too. She won't get away this time."

"I don't know, Jim," said his friend. "You know what Harold told you. They been looking for us in Whispering Springs. You stirred up a hornet's nest messin' with that gal and her sister in Morgan's. And that boyfriend o' hers almost caught you the other mornin'."

"Pete's right," said Randal, who was the third man in Morgan's that night. "Somethin' happens to her, they'll be after us for sure."

Jim, their pseudo-leader, looked at his buddies in disgust. "Cowards. Ain't no way they're gonna know we had anything to do with what happens to her."

"What makes you think she won't tell?"

"When I get done with her, she won't be tellin' nobody nothin'." Jim laughed, a bone-chilling sound that had Pete and Randal looking at each other in alarm.

* * * * *

While Hayley was busy with her research, Jace fixed the lock on her door then called Logan, asking for a face-to-face council session. Logan invited Jace to come for lunch. When he arrived, Jace was surprised to find Bryn there as well.

He pulled Logan aside as Bryn led them into the kitchen. "Should she be here for this?"

Logan gave his friend a reassuring look. "I just had it out with Bryn for keeping secrets from me. I'm not going to turn around and do the same. Besides, Hayley is her sister, Bryn's more likely to know how she might react. Having been in the same situation, she can probably give you some pointers on how to break it to her. I really think she could help."

Jace nodded thoughtfully. "You're right. Actually," he added with a growing smile, "I really don't need you at all. Get lost, would ya?"

"Yeah, right," Logan growled. "You think I'm going to leave my wife alone with a man of your reputation?"

"You won't let that poor woman have any fun at all, will you?"

The two of them entered the kitchen, both grinning. "If you two are finished slinging the bull around, let's put it on the table and eat. I'm starving," Bryn complained.

With an indulgent smile, Logan pulled out a chair for her. "Sit right down here, sweetheart. It'll be our pleasure to serve you."

Bryn sat and sighed with pleasure. "Now this is more like it."

While the meal was assembled, eaten and the cleanup attended to, they discussed the situation Jace found himself in. Once her shock wore off that Jace had accidentally turned Hayley, Bryn was able to give him some pointers that he might find helpful.

In the end it came down to a few simple facts. "Jace, no matter how you tell her, it's going to be a shock. For you guys, being born into a pack and growing up with the knowledge of who and what you are is just a fact of life. But for us? Oh boy." Bryn shook her head at the memory. "It's like walking into a strange place where reality has been suspended. Things you thought couldn't possibly exist are suddenly all too real. Be firm, be honest. Hayley's always been levelheaded, but she's also adventurous and imaginative, more so than I ever was. I think she'll get through the telling all right. I really believe once the shock wears off, she's going to love being a were."

Jace nodded and rose from his chair. "Thanks. To both of you," he added, giving Bryn and Logan equal credit. "This has been a big help. I still feel like I've got a rock in the pit of my stomach, but it's not rolling around as much."

Bryn gave him a smile and a generous hug. "It'll be okay. I just know it will."

"If I can do it, you can," Logan agreed. "I think I trained you well enough to handle this."

Jace rolled his eyes. "How do you put up with this arrogant dog?"

"He has quite a few redeeming qualities. They offset his flaws," Bryn commented, giving Logan a loving smile, which he returned.

"I can see I gotta get out of here before the mush gets too deep," Jace commented and headed for the door. "I'll call you later and let you know how it went. If I'm not too busy, that is," he said with a grin and waggle of his brows.

"Look who's calling who a dog," Logan complained.

Jace laughed and left in a much better frame of mind than when he'd arrived.

Chapter Nine

ဢ

With a sigh of extreme satisfaction, Hayley closed her notebook. She'd made considerable inroads on her research and was exceedingly pleased with the results. Gathering up her things and the book she'd originally come to borrow, she headed out the door. It was with some surprise that she noted the sun beginning its downward glide toward the horizon.

The previous three hours had passed with a speed she found amazing. "Too bad time doesn't go this quickly when you're doing something you don't enjoy," she muttered as she walked to her car.

Getting behind the wheel, she started the car and looked at the clock on the dash. With an hour's drive ahead of her, it would be nearly seven before she got home. At that moment, her cell phone rang. "Hello?"

"Hello there, beautiful. Where are you?"

Hayley grinned. "I'm still in Hibberd. I'm sorry. I found some great books and I lost track of the time. I know we said we'd meet this afternoon. I'll hurry."

"No, you *won't*. You *will* take your time and drive safe. How about we order pizza from Antonia's and eat in when you get here?"

"Mmm, that sounds wonderful. Thank you. You're a sweetheart."

"We aim to please, darlin'. I'll see you in about an hour."

"All right. Bye."

Hayley hung up with a warm feeling in her heart and a smile on her face. Jace really was a sweet, considerate man. There was so much more to him than a lot of people knew. She was so glad to be among the few who were given the chance to know the man who was hidden inside, the man she'd come to love.

She started the car and headed home. Driving the speed limit, she'd made about three quarters of the trip without incident, when the car began to sputter. "Oh no. What are you doing, baby?" She pulled to the side of the road as she lost speed.

The car coasted to a stop. Hayley tried restarting but there was nothing more than an odd grinding sound. "Damn!" she cursed with feeling.

She reached for her cell phone and called Jace. "Hey," she said, when he answered. "My car's stopped. I don't have a clue what's wrong with it. It won't start."

"Where are you?"

"I just passed the big farm that has the horse weathervane on the barn."

"The Dixon place. I know where you are. I'm about fifteen minutes away. I just came from giving the Buells an estimate for an addition to their house. Hold on, babe, rescue's on the way."

"Thank goodness," she sighed then turned at the sound of an approaching car. "There's a car coming. They're stopping." There was a moment's silence. "Oh no. Jace, it's that man. The one who broke into my house."

"Son of a bitch," Jace breathed. "Hayley, there's a big stand of woods right there. Run, baby. Hide in the woods. I'm coming. Do you hear me, Hayley? Run!"

Hayley stood frozen for a moment, staring at the man who'd promised to make her pay for humiliating him. She considered the possibility of taking him on until his two friends got out of the car. A cramp of pure terror twisted her stomach. One look at the odds was all she needed. She ran.

Behind her, she heard the sounds of shouting. The ordered curses to stop did nothing but encourage her to run faster. She made it into the woods and began dodging through the trees. Having managed to hold on to her cell phone, Hayley struggled to dial 9-1-1. A single thought kept repeating in her head. There was no way she was letting Jace face these three men on his own. Afraid to stop, afraid to even slow down, her divided attention cost her. She tripped over a low-lying tree branch.

Hayley scrambled and barely managed to keep her feet. Hands outstretched to catch a nearby tree branch, the phone went flying into the thick underbrush. Shaking, scared and angry, she held on to the branch until her knees regained their strength. She debated on trying to find the phone when a nearby noise caught her attention. With a whimpering growl of frustration, she ran. Her panicked flight took her deeper and deeper into the woods. She ran until a hitch in her side caused her to slow and stop. Crouching down, she tried to catch her breath, being as quiet as possible.

In the distance she heard the sound of raised voices. It almost seemed as though the men were arguing amongst themselves. She didn't know why and didn't care. It afforded her more time. Time for her to rest, time for Jace to get there. The voices became fainter until it was quiet. Ominously so. Hayley shivered, squelching the sudden need to run, to get away as fast and as far as she could.

Her body began to shudder. At first, she was able to convince herself it was shock until muscle and bone began straining in a way that was foreign and frightening. Clamping a hand over her mouth, she dropped completely to the ground and lay on her side, riding out the pain, rocking back and forth, her mind a morass of fear and confusion.

Something was moving inside her, something was coming alive, struggling to break free. Unfamiliar thoughts and images were forming in her head. Her senses were suddenly opened, as though released from a muffling cloak. The smell of the earth, grass and leaves wafted into her nostrils. A squirrel had recently passed over this ground and the thought produced longing. Longing to chase, to play, to hunt.

A fresh blaze of pain burned through her and she whimpered, helpless to keep the sound from leaving her straining throat. With the pain came stubborn determination. She would not be conquered. She was wild and free. This was her place, her turf, and no one would humble her. Slowly the pain began to ease.

Ears straining to catch any sound, she realized what it was to be prey and her psyche rebelled at the thought. Unbeknownst to her, her eyes began to glow. This was wrong! This was all wrong! She was the hunter, the predator. Why was she running? Breathing deeply, pushing the pain away, she rolled to her hands and knees then froze.

"Thought you could hide from me, did ya?"

Her enemy stepped from behind the trunk of an ancient oak. Hayley tensed.

"I told you I was gonna make you pay, bitch. Stay right there on your hands and knees. You're gonna gimme what you owe."

Warily, she watched as he approached, his hands working open his belt buckle. Hayley felt a growl forming in her chest. Softly she gave vent to the sound, her lips pulling back to show a hint of white teeth. When he opened the top button of his grimy jeans, she sprang. Taken by surprise, he went down under her attack. Biting, scratching and kicking, Hayley instinctively inflicted as much damage as she possibly could.

The man was yelling, rolling on the ground, struggling to catch hold of some part of the whirlwind of fury that was literally tearing him apart. He managed to get his leg bent and kicked out, catching Hayley in the stomach. With a whoosh of departing breath, she was sent flying and landed with a solid thump against a nearby tree trunk. Stunned, she lay there, gasping for breath.

Catching his breath first, the man scrambled to his feet. He reached behind to the waistband of his jeans and pulled a gun. Scratched and bleeding, he pointed the gun at her. "You are one crazy bitch. I'm getting the hell out of here. But you're not."

Just as he pulled the trigger, a huge shadow leapt between them. The black wolf clamped his teeth on the man's arm, crunching the bones in his powerful jaws. The man howled and once again was taken to the ground. The gun fell from his nerveless fingers as he slammed with jarring force against a fallen log. His head whipped back, impacting with the solid bulk of the tree trunk. Abruptly, his cries ceased as he was knocked unconscious.

A lifetime passed in mere seconds as Hayley stared in shock and surprise. The black wolf turned his gaze to her and she gasped. The blue-green of his eyes blazed. Hayley recognized the man within. "Jace," she whispered.

The air blurred around him. Hayley was assailed by a rush of vertigo as a transformation took place that was incomprehensible to the human eye. Where the wolf had been, Jace crouched. His magnificent body was nude. He rose unselfconsciously to his feet. Making sure the gun was out of her attacker's reach, should he regain consciousness, he moved swiftly to her side.

"Hayley," he said, his voice husky with emotion. "Are you all right?" He reached out, gently touching her face.

"You're a wolf," she answered. Still dazed, she breathlessly blurted the words.

Jace gave her tentative smile. "The accurate term is werewolf, but yeah, I can become the wolf. He lives in me."

Before she could reply, a swift lance of pain sliced through her. Hayley bent double as the insistent shift of bone and muscle again shuddered through her. Jace slid an arm around her shoulders. He was speaking softly. She strained to hear, to understand, but the words seemed almost alien to her.

When at last the pain receded enough to allow her to think, she looked at him, suspicion and accusation clearly written in her gaze. "What's happening to me?"

Subdued, Jace met her eyes. "It's the change, Hayley."

"What change?" her voice rose in panic.

"You've got to calm down, honey. That's why it hurts. You need to relax. Don't fight it."

Panting, Hayley growled at him, "You're not answering my question. *What* change?"

"You're becoming a werewolf. Like me," he admitted.

Hayley was shaking her head in denial.

"I'm sorry, baby. I'm so sorry. It was an accident. I would never have done this to you without your permission. That's part of what I've been wanting to tell you. About me, about this other side of me."

Disbelief, shock, fear and sudden rage coursed wildly through her. Her mind seemed to fragment, her thoughts jumbled. Some were clear, others unfamiliar, primitive and incomprehensible. Before she could make sense of it and speak, Bryn arrived with a wolf at her side.

Bryn knelt at Hayley's side. "Are you all right? Hayley, look at me," she ordered.

Hayley looked up at the command in Bryn's voice.

"It's all right, sis. It's gonna be all right."

"You know about this?" Hayley whispered.

Bryn nodded. She drew Hayley's gaze to the wolf. "That's Logan."

"Oh, Bryn." Hayley shuddered. "I can't believe this. I don't know what to say, what to feel, what to do. It hurts, it hurts so bad."

"You've got to let Jace help you," Bryn told her firmly.

"No! I don't want him. He did this to me. Make him go away!"

Stunned silence filled the little clearing.

Quietly, Bryn broke the silence. "Jace, Logan. Would the two of you give us some privacy? And take *that* with you, please," she added, indicating the man on the ground who remained still and quiet.

Logan transformed. He and Jace lifted the man to his feet and dragged him away.

Bryn turned back to Hayley. "Have I ever lied to you?"

"No," Hayley admitted in a shaky voice.

"Then listen to me now. I want you to sit there and relax. Take deep, slow breaths." When Hayley did as she asked, Bryn continued. "You've been given a gift, Hayley." At Hayley's look of disbelief, Bryn smiled. "Oh I know. You don't think so now. But in time, you'll believe me. It's not like in the movies. You don't become an unthinking, killing creature at the rising of the moon. *You* control the change." Bryn pitched her voice to sooth and calm. "Anytime you want, you can become the wolf. It's like nothing you'll ever experience. To run so swiftly you feel as though you could fly. Your senses come alive. The very air holds secrets, but they'll all be yours just by taking a deep breath."

"How?" Hayley whispered, shuddering as her body again sought to become that which it wasn't born to be.

"First of all," Bryn smiled. "You have to take off your clothes."

"Great," Hayley answered and Bryn smile widened into a grin.

She helped Hayley to her feet and out of her clothes. "Now, look into my eyes."

"You sound like a vampire. You're not going to bite me, are you?"

"Hey, that's just what I said to Logan! And no, I'm not going to bite you. Now do it."

Striving to put her fear aside, Hayley took a deep breath. Two pairs of silvery-gray eyes met. Almost immediately, Hayley felt her panic recede. Her body relinquished the remnants of its pain, flooding her with a feeling of peace and wellbeing. Deep in her sister's eyes, she saw the wolf. It stared back at her, claiming her, welcoming her, inviting her to join in the grace and mystery of its being.

Warmth enveloped her. Heat shimmered over her body and Hayley shivered with pleasure at the melting sensation that flowed over her. She shook herself then froze in shock. Instead of being face-to-face with Bryn, she was now at eye level with Bryn's thighs. She shied away, moving back while looking up, then sat abruptly.

Bryn looked down at her with a grin. "You make a beautiful wolf, sister of mine. We are going to have so much fun running together. I think it's time we show Jace and Logan the new you."

At the mention of Jace's name, a morass of emotion went spinning through her. Longing, confusion, need, anger—they mixed and mingled in an incomprehensible jumble. She heard Bryn call for them and watched the two men appear. Her gaze arrowed straight to Jace and she attacked.

Here was the author of her pain, spoke the wolf, and yet her humanity reminded her of the love she felt. Her front feet connected with Jace's chest, knocking him off his feet. He landed with a thud on his back and she stood over him, her jaws mere inches from his throat.

Bryn and Logan both cried out. "No!"

Back and forth, Hayley's human and wolf halves argued within her. Thoughts of love, betrayal, gratitude, hurt, longing for his touch and the need to inflict pain for pain raced through her mind as she stared down at the man at her mercy. Teeth bared, she growled at him in warning, daring him to move.

144

"Hayley, baby, I'm so sorry. I never meant to hurt you. I..." Jace swallowed hard. "I know I don't have any right to tell you this now, but...I love you."

The wolf froze. Slowly she relaxed, letting her growls abate. She stepped back, one step, then another, as she watched one crystal tear slide from the corner of Jace's eye. Horror at her own actions rolled over her in a wave. She lifted her muzzle to the sky and howled out her grief and shame. Sending one more look his way, she whirled and ran.

"Hayley!" Bryn yelled.

"Go after her, Bryn," Logan ordered softly. "Take her home. Jace and I are going to clean up this mess."

Bryn sent a worried glance in Jace's direction. He'd sat up but remained on the ground, his gaze trained on the spot where Hayley had disappeared. His expression was blank, his eyes held a bleak and weary resignation.

"Talk to him, Logan. This can't end this way. We have to fix this," Bryn insisted, her voice holding something akin to panic.

Logan wrapped her in his arms. "I know, sweetheart, I know. First things first. Go after Hayley. Take care of her. I'll see to Jace. It'll be all right."

"I hope you're right," Bryn replied fervently. She quickly stripped out of her clothes, handing them to Logan. "I'll see you at home."

"Be careful," Logan insisted, giving her a scorching kiss. "I love you."

"I love you back," Bryn answered with a misty-eyed smile. She transformed and followed Hayley's scent into the woods.

Logan moved to stand near Jace. Without looking up, Jace murmured, "It's over."

"It's not over 'til you're dead," Logan replied bluntly, drawing Jace's gaze to him. "You look very much alive to me. Come on, brother wolf," he reached down, extending his hand to Jace. Jace clasped his hand and allowed Logan to help him to his feet. "A lot happened here in a very short period of time," Logan told him. "Hayley was assaulted and confronted with information that was more than just mildly shocking. She's going to need some time. Give her that time, Jace."

Jace nodded, saying nothing, but deep inside he felt lost. Hayley's first act as a wolf had been to attack him. Could she have expressed her feelings more plainly? He closed his eyes and raised a hand to his forehead as though physically trying to erase the memory. And that look in her eyes before she ran away. The pain he'd caused her. How would she ever forgive him?

"Logan, how could I have fucked up so badly? I should have told her that first night I saw the change taking her. If I hadn't been such a coward—"

"Well, you can stop that bullshit right now. You are no coward, Jace McKenna. Just because you wanted to wait to be sure of Hayley's feelings? How long has it been? A few days? Come on, let's be realistic here. If this is what you're basing your idea of cowardice on, you don't have a leg to stand on. Now stop feeling sorry for yourself and help me with this bastard."

Jace's eyes took on a feral glow as his regard was drawn to Hayley's attacker. The unconscious man groaned and started to stir. "Why don't you go get our clothes and I'll walk this guy out to my truck."

Logan took one look at Jace's face. "I don't think so. You go get the clothes. I'll walk him out. And he rides with me to the sheriff's office."

"Sounds like you don't trust me."

"Let me put it this way. If this guy had attacked Bryn, I wouldn't trust myself. If that had been the case, would you trust me to be alone with him?"

Jace looked at Logan for a moment. "I'll go get our clothes."

"Smart man."

Jace remained in human form until out of sight, then transformed. Logan hauled the miscreant to his feet. "You have no idea how lucky you are at this moment," he growled. "Come on. You've got a date with the sheriff."

Logan herded the scruffy, subdued man toward the road.

* * * * *

Hayley stared into the koi pond, watching the fish make their graceful yet lazy rounds. Her thoughts moved in slow circles that emulated their movement. While they seemed content with the motion, Hayley was lost. A week had passed since she'd been attacked. Bryn and Logan had insisted she stay with them for a time. Her testimony, along with that of his two friends, had her assailant cooling his heels in jail. He was awaiting trial on charges of assault and attempted murder.

Any thoughts she had of her attacker and his part in the incident that took place in the woods was minimal. What held her attention most was Jace. Where he was, how he was, and how much she wanted to see him. But she didn't dare. Not after what she'd done, what she'd felt. Hayley was afraid. Ashamed of the way the way she'd nearly hurt him. There was nothing she could do but stay away.

At times her thoughts were still a confused tangle. She'd wake crying, unable to make sense of the morass of roiling emotions. Any peace she found was hard won but even so, inadequate. Happiness seemed a thing of the past, an emotion that might never return. She heaved a sigh and turned her head to see Bryn and Logan approaching from across the lawn. She moved over to make room for them on the stone bench.

"From the looks on your faces I see you think it's time for a talk. You may as well save your breath for all the good it will do," she told them, without looking up.

"Don't be a smartass," Bryn replied with some asperity. She knelt on the grass at Hayley's feet.

Logan seated himself on the bench beside her. "Haven't you brooded long enough?"

"I don't think so," Hayley replied with a tinge of annoyance in her voice.

"Too bad," Bryn answered. "It's time to talk."

"Bryn," Hayley began.

"No, I don't want to hear any excuses. I want to know how you feel. What's running through your head? Have you decided you don't love Jace?"

"Yes. No! Oh I don't know," Hayley returned forcefully. "You saw what I did. I attacked him. What does that mean? If I truly loved him, how could I have done that?"

"Wait a minute. Is that what has you upset?" Logan asked.

"Well, of course it is!"

Bryn and Logan looked at each other. "We thought it was the whole 'being a werewolf' thing."

Hayley frowned. "While I admit it's taking some getting used to, I don't see it as a real problem. If Bryn can handle it, I can."

"Well, thanks," Bryn replied sarcastically.

Hayley smiled for the first time in days.

"Then you're not mad at Jace?"

"No."

Logan rubbed his forehead. "All right, let's inject a little logic here. Hayley, what were you feeling when you attacked Jace?"

"Hurt, anger, gratitude, love. I don't know. It's all mixed *up!*" she wailed.

"Calm down," Logan urged and slid an arm around her shoulders. Bryn reached out and covered Hayley's hands with her own.

"The way I see it, there were two men in that clearing. Could it be that some of those emotions were meant for one and some for the other? Although we retain possession of our faculties when we transform, the wolf has a certain influence," Logan explained. "You'd been hurt. You were afraid when that man Jim attacked you. The gratitude you felt could have been aimed at Jace for the rescue. And hopefully, the love."

Hayley looked at him with dawning hope in her eyes.

"Wolves are intelligent creatures, but it's possible with so much happening so fast, everything became muddled. A confused animal often behaves with aggression. And Hayley, you didn't actually hurt Jace. You knocked him on his ass, true. But hey, who's to say he didn't deserve to be beat up a little. After all, he changed you without your permission."

"Logan!" Hayley and Bryn both protested his last statement. "That was an accident," Hayley defended.

Logan chuckled. "Don't you think you should tell *him* all this? Go put the man out of his misery. And I do mean misery. Cade and I are about at the end of our ropes. Jace is talking about leaving town. In fact, he mentioned something about taking off this afternoon."

"What!" Hayley cried. "That idiot," she whispered as tears filled her eyes. "I don't hate him, I love him."

Bryn squeezed her hands. "Go. Now. Tell him."

Hayley hugged first Bryn then Logan. "I will. Thank you, both."

Hayley rushed off. Bryn looked at Logan with a suspicious frown. "Did he really say he was leaving town?"

Logan gave her a wide-eyed look and nodded. "He mentioned it. Of course it was just to work on a job. He's coming back in a couple of days."

Bryn's mouth opened in shock, then a grin stole over her face. "*You* are diabolical."

"I'm not Pack Liaison for nothing. There's a certain amount of guile involved," Logan confessed with a smile.

Kate Steele

"Hmm, I'll consider myself forewarned."

"Would I use guile on you?" Logan asked innocently. "And by the way, did I tell you how beautiful you look today?" His eyes took on a soft golden glow.

"Logan. I told you I want to go to Hibberd. There's a store over there that sells baby furniture," Bryn rose and began walking toward the house.

"I know, sweetheart. I'm perfectly willing to go. I just thought we might delay the trip for an hour or so," Logan deliberately stalked after her.

Bryn increased her speed toward the house. "I don't know. Your hour or so has a tendency to turn into hours, plural."

"But, babe, you know I can't help it. Once I have you in my arms, you're all I can think about." Logan lengthened his stride.

"Baloney," Bryn accused and took off running.

Logan caught her easily and swung her up into his arms. "That's no baloney, love of mine. It's the whole truth and nothing but the truth." The kiss he gave her was long, deep and filled with passion.

Bryn came up panting for air, her eyes two pools of molten silver. "I guess we can go to Hibberd tomorrow," she conceded gracefully.

"You bet," Logan agreed and carried her into the house.

"But we *are* going tomorrow."

"Of course."

"Logan, I mean it."

"I know."

"Darn you."

"Now, Bryn…"

Chapter Ten

∽

"So what are you going to do?" Cade asked the question as he and Jace strolled the grounds surrounding Jace's house in the woods.

Jace shook his head in agitation. "Logan said give her time. It's been a week now and it's killing me. I've got the Williams job to take care of, I was going to hand it over to you but I need the distraction. When I get back I'm going to try to see her. I can't stand this any longer."

"I understand how you feel," Cade commiserated.

"The cast-iron bitch?"

"Yeah."

They ended their stroll in front of Jace's house and seated themselves on the edge of the porch. "You never did tell me what happened there. I take it this woman was important to you?"

"Guess you could say that."

"Well, you did say you loved her."

"I loved her once. A long time ago," Cade replied. "Sometimes things don't work out the way we hope they will. I don't expect this situation to change."

Jace sighed. "Damn. What is it about women? They sure can turn a man inside out."

Cade snorted a soft laugh. "Ain't that the truth."

At that moment a car made its appearance, slowly following the long, winding drive. They watched in silence as the sporty, black BMW came to stop. The door opened and a woman stepped out. Jace heard Cade take a long indrawn breath and felt tension fill his beta.

The woman was medium height with long, wavy dark hair that flowed freely over her shoulders and down her back. Even from a distance, Jace could see the sapphire glint in her eyes. She was dressed in a conservative black suit with a jacket and matching skirt that accented her generous curves. She walked toward them on black high-heeled shoes.

"You know her?" Jace asked as she approached.

"Yeah," Cade answered, his voice becoming careful and controlled. "That's the cast-iron bitch."

"Whoa," Jace commented. "She looks pretty cushy to me."

Cade gave him a quelling look and rose to meet her. "Delilah Christensen, as I live and breathe," he drawled. "What are you doin' here in the boonies, darlin'?"

"You know why I'm here, Cade," she replied in a smooth, cultured voice. "You're my mate."

"Go home, Del. Nothing's changed. I'm *not* putting myself under your daddy's thumb. I refused that, um...*opportunity* four years ago," Cade answered. His voice was heavy with sarcasm. "I'm not about to succumb now."

"I know you're not. But you're wrong about nothing changing. I've changed. I want to be with you."

There was a moment of silence. "Too late, darlin', but thanks for the offer. By the way, this is my alpha, Jace McKenna. Jace, Delilah Christensen," he said, introducing them. "Jace, things are gonna work out for you and Hayley. Some things are meant to be." He turned back to Del. "While others aren't. I'll see you, Jace."

Without a backward glance, Cade got in his Corvette and drove away.

Jace and Delilah watched him go. She stood tapping her foot for a moment then muttered, "If he thinks he's going to get away that easily, he's got another think coming." She turned to Jace. "I'm pleased to meet you, Mr. McKenna. I'm sure we'll be seeing more of each other. I've bought a house in Whispering Springs. No matter what Cade says, I'm staying."

Jace smiled. "Well, that's good news, I guess. But it looks like you've got your work cut out for you."

Del smiled in return. "Don't I know it. What is it they say? Anything worth having is worth working for?" She sighed. "I'm in for some hard labor. Oh well, good day, Mr. McKenna," she said and turned to walk toward her car.

"Call me Jace," he called after her.

She seated herself behind the wheel and rolled down the window, "Thank you, Jace. I'm Del." With a wave, she took off, following Cade's retreat.

"Well, isn't that somethin'?" he muttered and turned to go in the house.

A few minutes later another car came speeding down the lane. It screeched to a halt in front of the house amid a cloud of dust.

"What the hell?" Jace muttered and went for the front door.

Just as he opened it, Hayley appeared and without waiting for an invitation stalked passed him and into the house. She stared at the suitcase that waited at the bottom of the stairs. "It's true. You're *leaving*. How could you?" she accused, her silvery gray eyes flashing with ire.

"Hayley, I—"

She put up her hand. "I don't want hear it, Jace McKenna. I can't believe you're just going to run away. I thought you'd fight for me. You said you loved me. Did you mean it or was it a lie?" Hayley watched as heat and anger filled his stormy eyes.

"I never lied to you. I admit I should have told you about myself sooner, but I didn't lie abut anything. I do love you, damn it!"

Hayley gave him a haughty look and walked into the living room. In front of the fireplace she began to unbutton her shirt. "Prove it," she challenged.

Jace followed, and ground out in a husky rasp, "Darlin', do you remember what I said about tempting a wolf?"

She shrugged out of her shirt and let it fall to the floor. "I remember. You said it was a dangerous game to play. I'm not playing."

She unbuttoned her jeans and lowered the zipper. With a sensual wiggle, she pushed them over her hips and down her legs. Not bothering with the buttons, Jace ripped open his own shirt. Hayley's eyes took on a silvery, feral glow and she sent him a smile filled with carnal invitation as she stepped out of her jeans.

Jace emulated her and rid himself not only of his jeans but his briefs as well. His cock was fully erect, hot, swollen and ready. Hayley let her gaze wander his sleek, muscular body. Reaching behind her back, she unfastened her bra and let it slide down her arms. She took a few steps filled with a sultry sway toward him. Trailing her fingers over his body, she circled him.

"My mate," she murmured in a sensual, throaty voice.

Walking away from him, she gracefully lowered herself to her hands and knees on the rug in front of the fireplace. Looking back at him, she invited, "Mount me."

Jace tipped his head back and howled. The sound was deep, hoarse, raw and filled with hunger. Hayley had a moment's misgiving, until ancient, primitive needs and desires swept through her. Age-old urges took over before she could move and Jace was on her, his body covering hers. Without the slightest effort, he ripped her panties away.

"Down," he ordered.

With a husky, feminine growl, she complied, crossing her forearms while lowering herself on her elbows. Eagerly she presented herself to him, open and waiting to be fucked.

Instead of the cock she expected, she received an eager tongue. Hayley cried out and shuddered under the onslaught of his tasting. A few strokes of his tongue was all she received before Jace withdrew.

She moaned in frustration but obeyed when he urged her to spread her thighs wider. Sensing his movements, she waited for his cock but was again surprised when his arms wrapped around her thighs. Hayley came up off her elbows and sat up to look down and find Jace on his back under her. He'd positioned himself with his face at the apex of her thighs.

"Jace?" she questioned.

"Sweet, warm honey. Feed me," he growled.

"Oh God," Hayley groaned and lowered herself to him.

His lips and tongue eagerly burrowed in, parting the swollen petals of her sex. The sinuous movement of his tongue drove Hayley mad with need. She bounced above him, but Jace easily controlled her, keeping her right where he wanted her. He'd promised to feast between her thighs, and feast he did.

His tongue slid over her throbbing clit, petting, then rhythmically laving, until she was crying out and writhing above him. Feeling her orgasm approach, he switched tactics and plunged his tongue deep, drilling her wet, quivering channel while swallowing down the fresh cream that greeted his sensual maneuvers.

Hayley was lost, stunned by his actions. Unconsciously she cupped her breasts, kneading the full, fleshy globes as her hips undulated in Jace's grasp. His mouth and tongue played a wondrous game until, latching onto her clit with real intent, he sucked it between his lips.

Her orgasm burst free like a wild thing. She wailed and fell forward as her body shook and shuddered under the onslaught of sensation. Jace released her and slid out from beneath her. He rose and covered her body with his own, mounting her. His thick cock slid deep within her still-trembling channel. Hayley gasped and moaned at his entrance, helpless to do more than let the seething waves of pleasure sweep through her.

Jace began slowly pumping in and out. The convulsive clasp of Hayley's warm, wet cunt milked him. He grunted and continued to thrust against the pressure of muscles that massaged and encouraged his release. Determined to defy the siren song of her body, he was not ready, not willing, to let such rapture escape so quickly.

He rode her body, draping himself over her, covering her. "My woman, my mate, *mine*," he growled against her shoulder and bit down, holding her for his domination.

The salty tang of her skin tinged with the copper taste of her blood filled his mouth. Jace growled again as a red haze filled his vision. Hayley bucked beneath him. Her struggles and cries of passion enflamed him. His hips drove forward and back, the muscles of his ass bunching with each move. His cock powered in and out, full and deep, again and again until there was only flesh and heat and sweat and pleasure.

Mindlessly he fucked, wanting her release, needing her climax with a desire so strong it was impossible to ignore. He reached around her, his fingers finding her pussy. Parting the slick engorged lips, his fingertips found her clit. Settling the pad of one against the hard kernel, he began a quick, vibrating movement. Hayley's wail of release pulled a rolling growl from his chest.

A growing tingle slid the length of his spine. His seed-laden balls drew up. Hard and full, they smacked against the cushioning mound of her pussy. Those small, electrifying shocks merely added to his pleasure. A pleasure that finally became too great to deny. In a wave, his semen rushed the length of his cock and burst free, inundating Hayley's channel. Hard spasms clenched his insides, pulling him tight against Hayley with each spurt of seed that released. He clutched her hips, grunting at the sheer force of pleasure that knotted his gut.

Moments passed and the spasms eased. Jace released his grip on Hayley's shoulder and panted against her skin. Her scent swept over him in a wave and reality slowly returned. Her weakened shudders moved him to wrap his arms around her. Withdrawing from her, he turned her unresisting body in his arms. They collapsed in a graceful tangle of limbs to loll in silence, but for their panting breaths.

An occasional, barely audible whimper from Hayley brought Jace up on his elbow. "Are you all right? I didn't hurt you, did I?" he questioned with a worried frown, concern causing a renewed spark in his blue-green eyes.

"No, I'm not hurt," she answered in a breathless daze. She sighed, the sound sated and satisfied.

A tender smile curved his lips. "Rest a minute. Then we'll go upstairs so I can take care of you."

"I think you already did," Hayley replied. "My bones have turned to oatmeal. What's upstairs?"

"The bathroom, my bedroom. First I'm going to clean you up. Then I'm going to make love to you," he murmured, bending down to nuzzle her throat.

Hayley shivered. "I thought we just did."

"Oh no. That was a mating, hard and fast to satisfy the wolf. This is going be slow and easy, just for us."

Sudden tears filled her eyes. "Jace," she whispered. "The things you do to me. The things you make me feel. Sometimes it's just too much."

"Do you want me to stop, Hayley?" he offered, softly brushing the hair back from her face.

She wound her arms around him and pulled him close. "Never. Never stop."

"Never," he promised and sat up, pulling her with him.

Jace got to his feet and cradled Hayley in his arms. He held her possessively, easily climbing the stairs. His first stop was the bathroom. As promised, he put them both in the shower and tenderly washed her. The water was warm and refreshing. Hayley reveled in his attention. Moving at his direction, she ended up clinging to his shoulders as he backed her against the wall and let his fingers play between her thighs.

Just short of bringing her to orgasm, he urged her out of the shower where he dried her, then himself and led her to his bedroom. He lifted her, laid her down and joined her on the bed. The next hours passed in a sensual blur. Jace loved Hayley slow and easy. He caressed every inch of her skin. His large hands, slightly roughened by work, glided over her. Hips, thighs, buttocks and torso, all were explored over and over with equal depth.

His touch lit an ember that flared to a flickering fire and eventually became a raging inferno. Hayley moved to his touch, moaning softly as his fingers brushed her skin and gently kneaded the firm muscles beneath. He turned her to her stomach, stroking her back and buttocks. He let his mouth wander over her skin. Moving down her body, he gently nipped the full globes of her ass and smiled at her shivers.

Going further still, his mouth found the backs of her knees, which he kissed and laved with his tongue before sucking gently at the skin. Hayley whimpered and shook in reaction. Satisfied, Jace again turned her over and rose above her. He urged her to part her thighs and moved between them. Moving closer, he lifted her buttocks slightly to rest on his knees. He took himself in hand. His cock had thickened to bursting. The skin was tight and flushed, the plump head weeping thick, crystal tears.

His gaze held hers as he gently parted her delicate, swollen folds and fitted the head of his cock against her. He swept the throbbing head through her liquid silk, down to her entrance, then up to her clit, again and again. Hayley's lips were parted, her pants of anticipation coming faster when he slid inside that first small bit.

Ever so slowly, he entered. He felt the delicate, silky heat of her channel part for him as he eased inside. Hayley's legs lifted, wrapping around him, urging him to move faster, but Jace was determined. An eon later he was fully seated. He clasped her hands in his, raising them above her head while leaning forward to rest on his elbows.

"I love you, Hayley Royden," he whispered and took her lips with his own.

Their lips met and melded as their tongues languidly explored. Jace began a slow rocking movement that sent his cock sliding forward and back in an endless, unhurried pace. Their loving went on and on. His measured, deliberate thrusts wrung constant shivers from Hayley. Each diminutive orgasm had her shuddering.

Jace watched her. The delicate flush of her cheeks, the silver sparkle of her eyes. Her lips were swollen from his kisses, dewy and plump. Her tongue licked over the full curves as another soft moan issued from her mouth. Her nipples were a rosy red, engorged, the areolas puffy from his repeated suckling.

"Jace, please," she pleaded, her head tossing on the pillow.

"Do you love me, Hayley?" he asked softly.

"Yes!"

"Say the words. Please, Hayley, say the words."

Hayley smiled up at him, her lips trembling. "I love you, Jace McKenna. I love you."

Jace smiled in return. "That's all I need. That's all I'll *ever* need."

With those words he increased the pace. Thrusting deeper, harder, faster, he sent them both spiraling over the edge into the wild freefall of climax. Bodies heaving, arms clutching and holding, they rode the pleasure to its waning conclusion then rested together, drifting peacefully to sleep in each other's arms.

* * * * *

Hayley woke alone in Jace's bed to the sound of her own stomach growling. The smell of coffee and bacon wafted to her nostrils, bringing on another insistent rumble. She rolled out of bed and made a quick trip to the bathroom to take care of essentials.

Realizing she had nothing to wear, she opened the closet door in Jace's bedroom. She found a neat row of shirts and picked out a dark blue one. Following her nose, she found the kitchen where Jace, barefoot and wearing only a pair of jeans, was working at the stove. Softly she crept up behind him.

"I know you're there. I can smell you," he said, putting down the fork he was using before turning to take her in his arms.

"Great. I stink," Hayley groused.

Jace laughed out loud, his eyes sparkling with mirth. "Darlin', you far from *stink*," he claimed, burying his face between her shoulder and neck while taking a deep breath.

His action sent a shiver cascading down Hayley's spine.

"You smell so damn good, I can't get enough," he confessed in a husky rumble. "What are you doin' down here? I was gonna serve you breakfast in bed."

Hayley turned her head and kissed his cheek. "We can't stay in bed forever, you know. I was getting tired of being horizontal. I need a little vertical time," she teased.

Jace raised his head, giving her an impudent grin. "I can do vertical. You already know that."

She chuckled and returned his grin. "I know. But before you get too riled up, I think you better save your bacon."

"Oh shit!" Jace exclaimed and released her. He quickly transferred the bacon to a plate covered with paper towels. "Hayley, set the table, would you? The plates and things are in that cupboard over there and the silver's in the drawer right below it."

Hayley smiled and complied, liking the domesticity of it all. She set the table while Jace assembled the meal. He'd already made pancakes and had them warming in the oven. "How do you like your eggs?"

"Scrambled is good."

"Scrambled it is. Butter and juice are in the fridge and the syrup's in the cupboard here to my left," he instructed.

Hayley completed her tasks and a few minutes later the meal was ready and brought to the table. Jace poured coffee and juice before settling in his chair beside her. He watched Hayley take her first mouthful.

"Mmm," she murmured while chewing. She finished her first bite then told him, "You realize this is the second time you've cooked for me? I think we're setting a precedent here."

"I don't mind," he answered with a smile. "I've been on my own since I was nineteen. I learned to cook in self-defense, to keep from poisoning myself. But, um, *can* you cook?"

Hayley grinned at him. "I know my way around the kitchen. I'm no gourmet, but Mom saw to it that Bryn and I knew the basics. I have some recipes she sent with me. I make a mean beef and noodles."

"Sounds good. You know, there's a lot we don't know about each other."

"Are you worried you'll find out something you don't like?"

"No, more like worried you'll find out something *you* don't like."

Hayley gave him a look filled with understanding. "Jace, I love you. I think we've made it across some pretty high hurdles. Let's eat, then we'll talk. I want you to tell me everything that you're worried about. Logan said communication is the key, and I've learned how right he is."

Jace nodded and gave her a smile. "He's pretty good at that kind of thing. That's why he's pack liaison."

"Pack liaison?" Hayley questioned with a raised brow. "As in wolf pack?"

"Oh, darlin', we are going to have one interesting conversation."

"Oh *Lord*," Hayley groaned. Without another word she dug into her food like a prisoner enjoying her last meal.

* * * * *

A few days later, Hayley and Jace put in an appearance at Bryn and Logan's.

"I was beginning to wonder if you two were ever going to come up for air," Bryn teased.

The four of them sat, comfortable and relaxed, in Logan's den.

"I don't know why you wondered. You and Logan are still under," Hayley retorted with a grin.

Jace and Logan chuckled at their sisterly banter.

"So what have you been up to?" Bryn questioned innocently, then blushed scarlet at her words. "I mean, I know what you've been up to. No. Wait. That is… Well, crap."

Jace, Hayley and Logan burst out laughing and Logan hugged his mate to him. "We know what you mean, sweetheart."

Taking pity on her sister, Hayley stepped in. "We've actually spent a great deal of time doing something constructive." At Logan's raised brow, she smiled. "We've been talking. Jace has told me all about the Iron Tower and Twin Pines packs and the fact that you're pack liaison. Which, by the way, I think is pretty great. It's nice knowing my sister is marrying such a levelheaded guy."

"And how did you take the news about this new reality you've been thrown into?" Logan asked with a curious brow raised.

"She smacked me," Jace answered with a teasing gleam in his eyes.

"I did *not*, though I have some reservations about being the mate of an alpha. Everyone knows they're bossy know-it-alls," she retaliated with a smile. "Did you really have to fight for Logan?" She asked Bryn earnestly.

Bryn frowned at the memory. "I tried to, but two pushy alphas got in the way."

"Now, Bryn," Logan began.

"Bryn, honey," Jace chimed in.

She held up her hand to silence them. "I know, *I know*. Lillian would have torn me up and Reece needed the confrontation with her to win her as his mate."

"That's right," Logan agreed, giving her an approving look.

"Still doesn't mean I *liked* it."

"Bloodthirsty wench," Logan teased.

"Speaking of which, has Jace taken you hunting yet?" Bryn asked. She glanced at Jace to find him shaking his head, trying to signal her to hush.

"No..." Hayley turned her gaze to Jace for a moment. He immediately subsided, giving her a look of total innocence. Hayley cocked a suspicious brow at him. "Hunting for what?"

Bryn didn't give him time to wiggle out of it. "Bunnies," she announced with a teasing smile.

"*Bunnies!*"

"Or deer or squirrels."

"Oh my God. Don't tell me *you've* been hunting."

"Yep. It comes naturally to wolves."

Hayley looked at Jace. "Something tells me we've got a *lot* more to talk about."

"I didn't say we'd covered everything," Jace replied, giving her an apologetic smile.

"I can see that," Hayley declared, her temper beginning to heat.

"Who wants coffee?" Logan interrupted, giving his friend a break.

Jace immediately grabbed the line Logan threw him. "I do."

"You ladies stay and relax, Jace and I'll fix coffee," Logan said, rising.

"Cookies?" Bryn asked with a hopeful smile.

He leaned down to kiss the top of her head. "Anything for you, sweetheart."

"What about you, darlin', is there anything you'd like?" Jace asked Hayley cautiously.

Hayley studied him for a moment and felt what little ire that had been stirred by the conversation melt away. She shook her head. "I've got everything I need," she answered softly.

A grateful smile curved Jace's lips. "Same here, darlin', same here."

Bryn sniffed and the two of them looked at her. Her eyes were shiny with welling tears. "That is *so* beautiful."

Hayley shook her head and laughed. She rose and settled by Bryn, throwing an arm around her shoulders. "No more beautiful than you and Logan. Go on, guys. My sister and I need some privacy," she explained gently. "What's wrong?" Hayley asked, once the guys had made their exit.

"Nothing. I'm just really happy for you. When you told us about Steve, I hurt for you."

"Oh, Bryn," Hayley replied, truly touched. "Steve was a disappointment, I'll admit, but I didn't suffer anything near the pain that asshole ex of yours put you through. Seeing you with Logan has given me such joy. And as for me, I wouldn't change a thing. It all led to Jace, and I couldn't be happier."

The two of them hugged and shed a few sentimental tears before laughing at themselves.

"Have you and Jace talked about marriage or having children?" Bryn asked.

Hayley smiled indulgently and shook her head. "Give us a little time, sis. We're just getting to know each other. I'm sure we'll get around to all that." She gave Bryn a considering look. "Speaking of getting married, when are you and Logan going to do the deed?"

"I thought we already did," Logan interrupted before Bryn could answer. He and Jace had returned with coffee and Bryn's requested cookies.

"Not *that* deed. The wedding deed," Bryn answered, sending a quelling look in his direction.

"Oh. Three months. November third. You guys coming?" he announced with a teasing gleam in his eyes.

"November third!" Hayley exclaimed.

"Hell yes, we're coming," Jace replied with a disgruntled growl.

"That's good, 'cause you're my best man. If you'll accept the job?" Logan questioned with a hopeful smile.

A delighted grin broke over Jace's face. "'Bout time you asked me, you bastard." The two of them laughed as Jace pounded Logan on the back.

Bryn was shaking her head. "It must be a man thing, this lack of finesse. Hayley," she addressed her sister calmly, "Logan and I have decided to get married on November third. I'd very much like you to be my maid of honor."

"I'd be honored, Bryn," Hayley replied with a smile and a sparkle in her eyes as she went along with Bryn's formality.

"See, that's how you do it properly," Bryn instructed.

"Must be a girl thing," Logan answered, shooting Jace a grin.

"Yeah, but you know? Some girl stuff I'm beginning to appreciate," Jace replied, his loving gaze fixed on Hayley.

"Oh man. He's gone," Logan lamented. "Who was it, not so long ago I might add, who was saying something about the mush getting too deep? I think I need some waders."

Jace just smiled as Hayley returned his grin. He was indeed gone.

Chapter Eleven

ဢ

Three months later, on a briskly cool evening in November, Hayley and Jace were returning home. Bryn and Logan's wedding had gone off without a hitch. Logan's parents had returned several weeks earlier and spent time getting to know their future daughter-in-law and her family. Bryn and Hayley's parents had been there for the past week, staying at Bryn's old house. There was plenty of room now that Hayley had moved in with Jace.

As the car rolled slowly up the driveway, the headlights swept over the area and glinted off the front windows of the house. Falling leaves skittered across the lawn as the short grass bent under the gentle breeze. Soon winter storms would move in and Hayley dreamed of nights in front of the fire with Jace.

Her hand rested on his thigh and she gave it a gentle squeeze. "Everything went so well," she said with a happy sigh. "Didn't Bryn look beautiful?"

"She did. It's a shame her maid of honor almost outshone her," he teased.

"Well, it wouldn't be right to draw attention from the bride. But only *almost*?" Hayley asked wistfully.

"In my eyes, darlin', you shine like the sun."

"Oh, Jace," Hayley's voice quivered with suppressed emotion.

He parked the car and silently got out, walking around to open her door. Jace helped her out and slid his arm around Hayley's shoulders, quickly guiding her up the front steps and inside out of cold. A dim light shone on them from the living room, and there in the hallway, Jace took her in his arms and kissed her. Hayley wrapped her arms around him and gave back, heat for heat, need for need and love for love. When he broke the kiss, Jace's eyes were glowing. Hayley's reflected his perfectly.

"Marry me, Hayley. I love you. I want to make babies with you. Now. Tonight."

"You mean?" Hayley touched her stomach.

"You're ovulating again, sweetheart. You smell so sweet and ripe. I feel like the big bad wolf. I'm ready to eat you up."

Hayley took a breath to reply, when a sudden smell set the hair rising on the back of her neck.

"Well, ain't that sweet," came a reply out of the darkness, heavy with sarcasm. "Nobody would believe me when I told 'em about you bein' a werewolf. They all thought I was crazy." Jim Beeman, dressed in hospital scrubs, stepped forward into the dim light. He held a gun in his hand. "So I let 'em believe it."

"No," Hayley whispered as a thrill of fear swept through her.

Jace took a half step forward and tried to ease Hayley behind him, but she followed and stood fast at his side, sending him a glare. Jace sent her an exasperated warning glare in return. "How'd you get out of jail, Beeman? I thought they had you locked up tight." He shifted a bit in front of Hayley.

"Both of you just stand right there," Beeman warned. "And to answer your question, that's the beauty of bein' crazy. I got transferred to a mental ward. Some fancy doctor took a likin' to my psy...my psy..."

"Psychosis?" Jace supplied.

"That's the word," Jim admitted with happy nod. "I played along. I was the ideal patient. *Well behaved and cooperative*, Doc Henderson said. Too bad I had to hit him over the head like I did. I kinda hope he ain't dead."

"That's very generous of you," Hayley intoned sarcastically.

"You shut up, bitch! It's all your fault I'm in this mess. You and that uppity sister of yours. All you had to do was take it like a woman's s'posed to. I'da taken my due of pussy and gone on my way as usual. But no, you was just *too* good. So now I'm gettin' my due in another way. I'm gonna shoot me a genuine werewolf," he added proudly. "My old pappy, may he rot in hell, used to tell me stories about werewolves when I was a kid just to scare me. But I ain't stupid. I *know* that wolf was you. I still got friends on the outside. I learned all about you, *Mr. Jace McKenna*, and I got silver bullets in this here gun."

Hayley gripped Jace's arm. "That's murder. They'll put you away forever."

"Ain't no murder, shootin' a wolf," Jim denied. "Now, how's about you take off them fancy duds and turn into a nice doggy?" Jim turned the gun in Hayley's direction. His expression turned mean and ugly. "Or should I just shoot her right now?"

Jace growled. "Hurt her and you're dead."

Jim sorrowfully shook his head. "That ain't polite," he said and pulled the trigger.

Jace leapt in front of Hayley, his body jerking as the bullet struck home. Hayley screamed, the impact of Jace against her sending them both to the floor. A split second later, all hell broke loose. There were splintering crashes as several of the living room windows shattered. Through those broken windows, a pack of enraged wolves boiled in.

Jim Beeman screamed and went down under the combined weight of the infuriated, furry mass of bodies. His scream ended abruptly, the silence punctuated by growls and Hayley's panicked voice.

"*Jace*! Oh God, Jace. Don't be dead. Somebody help us!" She cradled Jace in her arms. His face had gone white, his eyes closed. Blood soaked the front of his tux jacket.

Outside, several vehicles arrived, including the sheriff. Inside, some of the wolves had taken their human shapes and were gathering around the couple on the floor. One wolf, still in animal form, threw its head back and howled. The sound was blood chilling and melancholy.

"Let me through," a voice ordered.

Logan knelt at Hayley's side. "Hold on, little sister. Hold on. Let Dr. Maigrey through," he ordered the crowd.

"Logan," Hayley whispered. Shock had her shaking, her voice unsteady.

A man she'd never met dropped to one knee on the floor beside them. "Let's see what we've got here," he said in a steady, businesslike tone.

Dr. Maigrey pulled scissors from his medical bag and cut away a portion of Jace's jacket and shirt, exposing the wound. He cleaned the area to reveal the entry point and found that the bullet had hit the fleshy part of Jace's shoulder. "Well, that's not too bad," he commented.

"Not too bad! That maniac shot him with a silver bullet!" Hayley shouted in outrage.

"I can see that, young lady," he said in a soothing yet authoritative voice. "In case you've failed to notice, the wound is smoking. Now hush and let me get that bullet out of him before it does any real damage."

Working with quick, steady efficiency, he poured a disinfectant on the wound that brought a wince and a groan from Jace, who was slowly coming to. "Hold steady now, son," he warned. "Logan, Cade, hold his shoulders. And get me some light in here." Hayley was gently muscled aside as the two men held Jace in place. Everyone blinked as the overhead lights flared on.

Another car pulled up outside and Bryn dashed in. "Hayley!"

"Here! I'm here, Bryn," Hayley called out and a worried Bryn dropped to her knees beside her.

"Are you all right?"

"I'm okay, but Jace was shot."

"How bad is it?"

Logan looked around. "He's going to be all right," Logan told her. His reassurance was meant not only for Bryn but Hayley as well. "Doc's just gotta get the bullet out." He turned back and Bryn took Hayley's shaking hand, holding it tightly.

Using a long probe, Dr. Maigrey found the bullet and began to ease it out. Jace was groaning, his face scrunched in pain. "Where's Hayley? Is she all right?" He started to struggle against Cade and Logan's hold.

"Hold still," Logan ordered. "She's right here and she's fine."

Jace subsided with a groan.

"Almost there, Jace. Your body's already trying to heal itself." As gently as possible, Dr. Maigrey pulled the bullet from Jace's flesh. "There now," he said, dropping it to the floor. He poured more disinfectant into Jace's wound.

"Son of a bitch, Doc! Did you have to do that?" Jace complained around clenched teeth.

"Just a precaution, son, just a precaution. You fellows carry him into the living room and lay him on the sofa." Dr. Maigrey followed behind them, giving orders as they went. "I want you to lie there for at least half an hour. You hear me? No vigorous exercise for the next twelve hours, get some food in you and drink plenty of fluids. Give your body time to recoup the blood loss."

His orders were carried out. Jace was safely ensconced on the sofa with Hayley kneeling by his side when the cleanup started. After a few minutes of waiting to see that he was all right, Hayley went for a washcloth. She helped him out of his ruined coat and shirt and gently washed away the remaining blood.

The sheriff, who was fortunately a member of the Twin Pines pack, got an unconscious Jim Beeman safely under guard and ensconced in an ambulance. He was to be returned to the psychiatric ward of the hospital with the recommendation that he be placed in a more secure facility. Charges were already being filed against him for his escape and for the assault on Dr. Henderson.

"When we file a second set of charges against him for attempted murder, not to mention breaking and entering and unlawful possession of a firearm, he'll be going away for a long time. I don't think his 'psychosis' is going to help him this time," the sheriff assured them before he left.

Most of the pack members—after assuring themselves of their alpha's returning health—took their leave, a few staying behind to help put things in order. The glass from the broken windows was swept up and plywood sheets nailed over the outside frames to keep the weather out until the glass could be replaced. Logan directed the work while Bryn went to the kitchen to heat up some tomato soup and make toasted cheese sandwiches.

Jace lay still on the couch, his uninjured arm around Hayley. She laid her head on his shoulder, her hand resting on his torso. Neither of them spoke. They were content to let events play out around them as everything grew quiet. Logan said goodbye and thank you to his helpers and Bryn brought the soup, sandwiches and glasses of milk out of the kitchen.

She set the tray on the coffee table. "Let's eat."

"I'm not hungry," Hayley murmured.

"Dr. Maigrey said Jace needs to eat. You've had a shock. You need to eat too. Come on, sit up. Let's see your face, girl," Bryn ordered.

Hayley sat up shook her head, giving Bryn a weak smile. "Bossy."

"Darn right. Help Jace with his food. Logan, help Jace sit up."

"I got it," Jace groused, easing himself upright. "I'm not an invalid, you know. This'll be totally healed in a couple of hours."

"Yeah, yeah, yeah, I know. The big strong man's no weakling," Bryn teased, then suddenly started crying.

"Bryn! Baby, it's all right," Logan crooned and gathered her in his arms. He sat down in an overstuffed chair near the sofa. Pulling Bryn down on his lap, he cradled her against him as he turned to Jace. "The sheriff called right after you two left. He told us about Beeman's escape and that he'd been tracked to this area. We tried calling, but there was no answer here or on your cell. Bryn was pretty worried. Hell, we both were."

"I didn't bother to bring the cell and we took a little drive before coming home," Jace explained. "I'm sorry you were worried. But I'm sure as hell glad you showed up when you did. Bryn, honey, you okay?" he asked gently.

Bryn raised her head from where she'd hidden her face against Logan's shoulder. "I'm all right. I just needed to fall apart a little." She rose from Logan's lap and went to Jace. Cupping his face in her hands, she kissed first one cheek and then the other. "Thank you for keeping Hayley safe."

Jace smiled. "Hey, that's part of my job. Now about that food. I'm kinda hungry."

There were smiles all around and everyone dug in. Hayley helped Jace, feeding him bites of toasted cheese sandwich dipped in his mug of soup. As soon as the meal was finished, the dishes were consigned to the dishwasher and Bryn and Logan took their leave. Bryn offered to cancel their honeymoon trip, but Jace and Hayley talked her out of it, much to Logan's relief.

They stood in the doorway and waved them on their way. Jace closed the door. "Are you all right, Hayley?"

"I'm fine. I'm not the one who got shot, you know."

Jace cupped her chin in his hand and gave her a searching look. "I know, thank God. It's just... You've been awful quiet."

She smiled at him and cupped his cheek. "It's been a crazy night. I'm just tired and you should be off your feet. I think bed's the best place for both of us."

Jace wiggled his eyebrows. "Now you're talkin'."

"We're going to sleep. Dr Maigrey said no vigorous exercise for twelve hours," she looked at her watch. "By my calculations, you've got nine and a half hours to go."

"Then I guess I'll go to sleep," he grumbled. "At least the time will pass faster that way."

Hayley chuckled. "You're incorrigible. Come on."

At Hayley's insistence, they took the stairs at a slow, careful pace. After a quick cleanup, they settled in bed together. Jace rested on his side, spooned against Hayley's back with his injured arm draped over her. It wasn't long before sleep found them. For a time.

Jace woke as Hayley tried to ease away from him. "Where you goin'?" he questioned groggily.

"I have to use the bathroom. I'll be back in a minute," she answered and slipped away.

Jace dozed until a soft sound woke him. He felt for Hayley and found her side of the bed empty, the sheets nearly devoid of any residual warmth from her body. Silently he rose and went to the bathroom, quietly opening the door. Hayley was on the floor, a towel jammed against her mouth as she rocked back and forth with tears streaming from her eyes.

With a deep rumble of distress, Jace sat on floor with her and encircled her with his arms and legs, pulling her back against him. "Shh, baby. Hush now, it's all right," he crooned softly while gently rocking her back and forth.

Hayley dropped the towel and turned her head into his shoulder, shuddering as she cried. Jace held her and rocked, murmuring words of comfort. When he tried singing, Hayley choked back a sob that had suddenly turned into a hiccupping laugh.

"I knew that would get you," Jace murmured against her temple. "Cade says I can't carry a tune in a bucket."

She gave him a watery smile. "I'm afraid he's right." She reached up to gently stroke his cheek. "I almost lost you," she said in a stricken whisper.

"Almost doesn't count, Hayley. We can't let almost get us down. We've got a lot to look forward to, darlin'. You *are* going to marry me, aren't you?"

"Of course I am," she admitted softly.

Jace beamed. He looked at her watch. "And in a few hours, we're going to start our family. We're going to watch our child grow here inside you," he said softly, his hand resting lightly on her belly. "Come on. You're cold," he said, rubbing his hands up and down her arms. "Let's go back to bed."

He helped her up. Hayley gave him an uneasy look. "I'll be out in a minute, I have to blow my nose and wash up."

"I'll wait."

"*No.*"

"Why not?"

"I don't want to blow my nose in front of you."

"Darlin', you're standing there naked and *that's* not bothering you."

"*Jace!*"

"All right! I'll wait for you in bed. Best you get to it. If you take too long, I'm comin' back," he warned and walked away, grumbling something about the peculiarities of women.

A minute later, Hayley joined him in bed. Jace was lying on his back and she snuggled up to him, draping her arm over his torso. He wound his arm around her shoulders and hugged her close as she laid her head on her chest. "Everything come out all right?"

Hayley began to chuckle as Jace's chest shook with suppressed mirth. They lay together, their bodies vibrating with the joyous, carefree sound. Finally, Hayley was able to take a deep breath. "You're a nut. You know that, don't you?"

"Then we're well matched, sweetheart, 'cause I'm not the only one who's a little left of center."

Hayley smiled and yawned then rubbed her cheek against him. "That's true," she admitted before drifting off to sleep.

Jace hugged her close and joined her.

* * * * *

Approximately twelve hours after he was shot, Jace was awakened by a pair of hands and lips that were doing lusciously arousing things to his body. He groaned as his rising cock was engulfed by a warm, wet mouth. His hips moved, initiating a counter rhythm to the sliding strokes of Hayley's mouth

She worked him for a few minutes then released him, her hand taking the place of her mouth as she moved up his body and leaned over him. "Hi there," she murmured against his lips. "How are you feeling?"

"As good as new. What are you up to, darlin'?" he panted, riding the shudders of pleasure her stroking hand brought him.

"I'm tempting the wolf," she explained reasonably. "I'm told it's a dangerous game to play. Is it working?"

Jace raised a brow. "You can't tell?"

Hayley chuckled softly. "I though I was making progress, but I don't see any signs of danger. Just a big pussycat lying here getting stroked," she teased, squeezing the thick erection that filled her hand.

Jace gasped and broke free. Before she could say another word, Hayley found herself on her knees with Jace covering her.

It was her turn to gasp as his cock found her entrance. "Jace, what are you doing?" she moaned.

"Reminding my mate that I'm pure wolf and the only pussy in this bed is right here," he growled and thrust forward, filling her slick sheath with the hard, full thickness of his burrowing cock.

"*My* wolf," Hayley growled in return, pushing the rounded mounds of her buttocks tight against him.

Jace rumbled in her ear, "That's right, Hayley. Never forget. *Your* wolf, always."

The bed shook as their bodies moved together while heated words of love and desire were exchanged. Hayley and Jace mated, giving and taking pleasure as they enjoyed the rewards that resulted from tempting the wolf.

Also by Kate Steele

ഇ

About the Author

ഇ

Having been an avid reader of romance for years, and being possessed of an overactive imagination, Kate decided only recently to try her hand at writing. She discovered that, like reading, writing romance has become addictive. Whether writing about werewolves and otherworldly creatures or contemporary gay/erotic romance, she has found the perfect outlet and is thrilled to be part of the Ellora's Cave family.

Kate lives in a turn-of-the-century house located on three acres in the midst of Indiana farm country. Keeping her company is her family, dogs, and other assorted pets.

Kate welcomes comments from readers. You can find her website and email address on her author bio page at www.ellorascave.com.

Tell Us What You Think

We appreciate hearing reader opinions about our books. You can email us at Comments@EllorasCave.com.

Why an electronic book?

We live in the Information Age—an exciting time in the history of human civilization, in which technology rules supreme and continues to progress in leaps and bounds every minute of every day. For a multitude of reasons, more and more avid literary fans are opting to purchase e-books instead of paper books. The question from those not yet initiated into the world of electronic reading is simply: *Why?*

1. *Price.* An electronic title at Ellora's Cave Publishing and Cerridwen Press runs anywhere from 40% to 75% less than the cover price of the exact same title in paperback format. Why? Basic mathematics and cost. It is less expensive to publish an e-book (no paper and printing, no warehousing and shipping) than it is to publish a paperback, so the savings are passed along to the consumer.

2. *Space.* Running out of room in your house for your books? That is one worry you will never have with electronic books. For a low one-time cost, you can purchase a handheld device specifically designed for e-reading. Many e-readers have large, convenient screens for viewing. Better yet, hundreds of titles can be stored within your new library—on a single microchip. There are a variety of e-readers from different manufacturers. You can also read e-books on your PC or laptop computer. (Please note that Ellora's Cave does not endorse any specific brands.

You can check our websites at www.ellorascave.com or www.cerridwenpress.com for information we make available to new consumers.)

3. *Mobility.* Because your new e-library consists of only a microchip within a small, easily transportable e-reader, your entire cache of books can be taken with you wherever you go.

4. *Personal Viewing Preferences.* Are the words you are currently reading too small? Too large? Too… ANNOYING? Paperback books cannot be modified according to personal preferences, but e-books can.

5. *Instant Gratification.* Is it the middle of the night and all the bookstores near you are closed? Are you tired of waiting days, sometimes weeks, for bookstores to ship the novels you bought? Ellora's Cave Publishing sells instantaneous downloads twenty-four hours a day, seven days a week, every day of the year. Our webstore is never closed. Our e-book delivery system is 100% automated, meaning your order is filled as soon as you pay for it.

Those are a few of the top reasons why electronic books are replacing paperbacks for many avid readers.

As always, Ellora's Cave and Cerridwen Press welcome your questions and comments. We invite you to email us at Comments@ellorascave.com or write to us directly at Ellora's Cave Publishing Inc., 1056 Home Avenue, Akron, OH 44310-3502.

COMING TO A
BOOKSTORE
NEAR YOU!

ELLORA'S
CAVE

Bestselling Authors Tour

erridwen, the Celtic Goddess of wisdom, was the muse who brought inspiration to storytellers and those in the creative arts. Cerridwen Press encompasses the best and most innovative stories in all genres of today's fiction. Visit our site and discover the newest titles by talented authors who still get inspired - much like the ancient storytellers did, once upon a time.

Cerridwen Press

www.cerridwenpress.com

Discover for yourself why readers can't get enough
of the multiple award-winning publisher

Ellora's Cave.

Whether you prefer e-books or paperbacks,

be sure to visit EC on the web at
www.ellorascave.com

for an erotic reading experience that will leave you
breathless.